The Minstrel Boy

A Future History

By

Nigel Seed

www.nigelseedauthor.com

"To every man upon this earth, death cometh
soon or late;
And how can man die better than facing fearful
odds,
For the ashes of his fathers, and the temples of his
Gods."

From 'Horatius at the Bridge' by Thomas
Babington Macaulay

Foreword by Robin E Horsfall.

Former SAS soldier, hero of the Iranian Embassy.
Veteran of five tours in NI, and an active
campaigner for veterans rights.

"The Minstrel Boy" is a wonderful fast moving
thriller. It revolves around the now hidden truths of
the IRA. In his novel Nigel reveals an active world
of international gangsters intent on destroying their
own people. Nigel Seed's references to true events
brings back many of the terrible atrocities that
were carried out by the IRA during my time with
the Parachute Regiment and the SAS, 1972-1984.
Money is still raised in 'Irish' communities around
the world in the name of 'The Cause'. That money
still kills people.'

Dedicated to the Army and Police personnel
that struggled long and hard to maintain the peace
in Northern Ireland despite the
successive British governments that
hamstrung them at the time and have
betrayed them ever since.

It is also in memory of Sgt Stuart Reed of the
Royal Electrical and Mechanical Engineers, killed
in a landmine attack on his Land Rover near
Dungiven on June 24th 1972.

This book is a work of fiction. However, I have interspersed the fiction with chapters that detail actual atrocities that were carried out by IRA terrorists during "The Troubles" in Northern Ireland. I have largely given the actions during these atrocities to fictional people who take part in my story. The names are therefore made up, but the actions are not. In the final chapter I have detailed the real events, places and people that actually existed so that you, the reader, can judge whether I have done the situation justice.

Acknowledgments

We are all travellers in the wilderness of this world and the best that we can find in our travels is an honest friend.
-Robert Louis Stevenson

I have been blessed with a number of honest friends who have helped me by reading my book at the embryonic stages and giving me useful criticism. They know who they are, but they deserve a mention for putting up with me. I should also say that I have been extremely lucky to find a superb editor. Any errors that still exist in the book are where I have ignored her excellent advice.

The biggest debt though is to my wife who has lived this project with me and been supportive throughout, especially when I was struggling

Chapter 1

The slap across the back of his head took him by surprise. His glasses fell into the breakfast cereal on the kitchen table before him and he swore quietly.

"What was that for, Ma?"

"I've told you a million times not to sing those feckin songs in my house. Two husbands I've lost to that bloody stupidity."

"I wasn't singing anything, Ma."

He looked across the table at his sister for support. "You may not have been singing, Billy, but you were humming and that's the same thing for Ma."

"Ah, thanks a bunch, Mary. I thought you might have backed me up for once. Especially as it's your last day."

She grinned at him and took a bite of her toast. "You wouldn't want to be making me a liar, would you, Billy Murphy?"

He looked across the kitchen at his mother, who was by the sink now. "Sorry, Ma. I didn't even know I was doing it. I must have been thinking about the gig tonight."

"Huh. Gig, is it? Dire Straits do gigs. You sing feckin rebel songs in pubs around Belfast. Not really the same thing, is it?"

"Ah fair play, Ma, it brings in the extra cash and you never know when someone will hear me and give me my big break."

She put the dirty plate down on the draining board and looked at him intently. "It's about time you stopped dreaming of stardom, Billy. Get a proper job with real prospects, then maybe you can get Niamh to come back to you. That girl was the best thing that ever happened to you."

He slumped in his chair a little. "That's not fair, Ma. You know she's with Michael O'Leary now."

"And why's that, do you think? Because he's got a good job, that's why. He's making something of himself and he can buy her nice things. He can take her to nice places, not just sit her in a dirty pub to listen to you singing that crap."

"Good job, is it? He sells bloody carpets in a warehouse. The only reason he got the job is because his dad's the boss."

She grinned. "That's right, and when the time comes his dad will pass it on to him and he'll be the boss, while you still sing in backstreet pubs. Hell, you can't even afford a decent guitar."

Mary decided it was time she helped her little brother out. "Fair play, Ma. He brings in extra money and there's not many jobs now the shipyard is cutting back."

"That's easy for you to say, Mary Murphy. You'll be back in America tomorrow and I'll still be stuck in this house listening to this one talk about how he'll make it big one day."

"You know I'd help you both move to America, but you won't leave Ireland. And I know Connor has offered to help you move to Australia with him."

"And how am I supposed to choose between my children? If I go with you then Connor will be put out, and how can I leave this useless lump on his own?"

"Sure and Billy can go too."

"No country would take him. Not a qualification to his name and no work experience at all, so why would they?"

Billy picked his glasses out of the cereal and wiped them dry. He pushed the plate away and stood up slowly.

"Thanks for the vote of confidence, Ma. I'll see you before you go to the airport, Mary. I need to go and get some new strings for the guitar."

Mary watched her younger brother leave the room before she spoke to her mother. "Ma, you need to give him a break, you know. He didn't deserve that."

"Easy for you to say, Mary, love. You're away back to America and your nice life. You got away from this place and good on you for that. Now I need to motivate our Billy before he becomes one of the scum that live here and do nothing but drink and get into trouble."

"I know why you do it, Ma, but maybe there's another way with Billy. Just think about it, eh?"

"Maybe if he saw what you've got in America?"

"Send him over for a holiday. The apartment's not big, but he can sleep on the sofa for a week or two. I'll show him round."

"I'll think about it, and you'd better finish your packing if you want to be ready for the taxi."

Chapter 2

Billy sat himself down on the bar stool that had been put on the small stage for him and tuned his old guitar. He looked around the room and thought about what Ma had said before Mary left for America. The usual drunks were here already and looked like they had been in the bar since it opened. The scarred wooden tables and chairs around the stage were mostly empty and he hoped they would fill up before he was due to sing. Singing to a room with nothing but three drunks and an old dog would be embarrassing, and not for the first time.

He set the guitar down at the back of the performing area and went over to the bar. "Expecting many folk in tonight, Ardan?"

The barman shrugged. "Got the regulars here and there'll be a few more of those in a bit. Surely your adoring fan club will be beating the doors down any minute, eh, Billy?"

Billy forced a smile he didn't feel. "You must have been talking to Ma. She thinks I'm wasting my time as well."

"Oh fair play, Billy. I didn't say you was wasting your time, now, did I? You're a good singer right enough, but playing in places like this is going no place fast. Maybe you should try your luck in Dublin or maybe Liverpool?"

"And with no job how would I eat while I'm in the big cities? These gigs don't pay much, even if I pass the hat at the end."

The barman shrugged again. "Up to you, Billy, mate, but you need to do something different if you want to make something of this singing. Staying around here will do nothing for yez."

"And what about yourself then? Is standing behind this bar the answer to your dreams?"

Ardan put down the glass he had been wiping and looked Billy in the eye. "No, Bill. I know this place is a shithole, but what choice do I have? There's no feckin work now that the shipyard is cutting back, and with my record, who the hell else will give me a job?"

Billy nodded slowly. "A drug rap will do that for you."

"Don't you be a smartarse, Billy Murphy. I get enough of that crap at home. You know damn fine I was only carrying that stuff cos the boys made me. Didn't want to end up in a back alley somewhere like your da."

"Then maybe you should take your own advice and get the hell out of Belfast."

Ardan smiled. "Maybe I should. You ever need a roadie, you give me a call. Anyway, it's time you were on stage. The posters we put up said you'd start now and you wouldn't want to keep your audience waiting, would you?"

Billy looked around. There was a young couple at one of the tables now, and an older man sitting alone behind a pint of Guinness, with his back to the wall. He took his drink and walked between the tables to the stage. The room looked more depressing that ever with just the three people in. He picked up the battered guitar and sat on the stool before tapping the microphone again.

"Well, good evening, folks. Lucky you came early to get a seat. We'll be packed out any minute, no doubt. If you want to sing along with any of my songs you're very welcome and if there's anything special you want to hear, then just let me know."

Nobody reacted and he looked down at the strings as he strummed a few bars. Maybe if people in the street heard the music they would come in. That worked sometimes, but on a cold rainy Belfast night with the wind blowing off the Irish Sea there wouldn't be many out for a stroll.

He started to play and sang them the old favourite, 'The Rising of the Moon'. That usually got their feet tapping, but tonight seemed different. The young couple on their date ignored him and carried on with their intense conversation. The man against the wall watched him silently and sipped at his beer now and then.

By the time he finished his first set the crowd had swelled by two more people. They listened to a song or two and then lost interest and had their own conversation. He finished the last song of this session and sat for a moment or two to see if there was any applause. There wasn't. He sighed quietly to himself and walked to the bar to get a refill.

As he passed, the older man waved him over and pointed to a chair. Billy sat down and looked the man over. He must have been at least sixty years old, but looked in decent shape for his age. His hair was white and thinning on the top, but his eyes were still clear and he wore no glasses.

"So you're Seamus Murphy's boy, eh?"

"So they say."

The man chuckled. "Seamus was a good friend of mine. It was a crying shame him being killed like that. I'm Patrick Flaherty, by the way, but everyone calls me Paddy."

"Nice to meet you, Paddy. How'd you like the songs?"

Paddy leaned his chair back on to two legs against the wall. "You sing well, boy, but you aren't getting the crowds in, are you?"

Billy glanced around the bar. "Not tonight, but it's cold and wet so maybe people want to stay in and watch the soap operas in the warm."

"You don't make much, singing in a dump like this, I'm guessing, and there's a lot of dumps like this in Belfast. You don't have a day job, do you?"

"I do all right on a good night. When I get the people singing along and then pass the hat. And there's bugger all work going round town right now."

Flaherty looked at him for a long moment. "If you want work then maybe I can help. How would you like to work for me?"

"Doing what and why me?"

"Singing, of course. I'm what you might call a fundraiser these days and I'm setting up a wee tour to go and find those funds. As to why, well I guess I owe yer da for a few favours and maybe I can pay back through you."

"A tour? Where would that be to then?"

"Oh, we might start in Liverpool and Manchester. Then, if they go well, we're off to Boston and New York and any number of other places."

"New York? Are you serious? You want me to go to New York?"

"That's right, Billy boy, and it's all in a good cause. What do you say?"

Billy thought for a moment, then leaned on the table. "So who pays for all this?"

"I have some friends who'll set us up. Then, when the fundraising kicks in, we take our expenses from that before we send the lion's share to the cause."

"So it's just you and me on this jaunt then?"

"Mostly, yes, but there's always friends in the places we are going who'll lend a helping hand. So what do you say?"

Billy looked around the pub again and took in the bored people and the peeling paintwork. He looked back at Flaherty, who was waiting patiently for his answer.

"I can't just swan off around the world; I'll need to speak to me ma."

"So? What are you waiting for? If you need her permission, go call her now. See if she'll let her little boy go on an adventure."

"It's not about permission. If I go she'll be on her own while I'm away."

Billy had considered telling him to go to hell, but the prospect of singing in the US had his attention. He rose from the table and walked outside where he could not be overheard. He was

15

surprised at how quickly his mother agreed to him going. She didn't even ask how much he would be paid. He walked back inside, putting his mobile phone back in his pocket, and sat down.

"When do we leave?"

Chapter 3

"You're sure I shouldn't have bought a new guitar for this then?"

Flaherty nodded and put his drink down. "I'm certain. We need you on stage looking the part."

"I think it's time I asked what part and who is it we are collecting for anyway?"

Flaherty smiled. "You wait until we are in the departure lounge at Manchester airport before you ask who we are doing this for."

Billy nodded. "That's right. Whatever happens now I get a trip to New York. You can't throw me out of here without a huge fuss with the security people."

"Sneaky little bastard, aren't you? Well, all right then. What we are raising funds for is the final push to achieve a united Ireland."

"Oh, come on now. Surely that's dead and buried? The IRA campaign lasted for bloody years and got Sinn Fein into government at Stormont."

Flaherty picked his drink up from the table and sipped it before he spoke. "The cause of Irish freedom never dies, boy, but we've been playing the long game and now the time is ripe."

Billy leaned back on the uncomfortable airport chair. "Go on then, I'll bite. What the hell is the long game when it's at home?"

"Oh ye of little faith. You must have seen all the stuff in the newspapers about British army men being prosecuted for killings done in the 1970s? Best part of fifty years ago now, but we are going to drag them into court and with a bit of luck we'll jail a few of them."

"Two questions then. Who's we, and why?"

"Sinn Fein has been putting people into key positions for years. Now we've got IRA sympathisers in the police and in the prosecution service at senior levels. The 'why' is easy. First, it's revenge, and secondly, and more importantly, it damages the morale of the army today. They will be less effective when they see that the British government will throw them to the wolves for obeying their orders. On top of that, the army has been reduced in size by the government to save money, the cheap bastards. So if the troubles kick off again the army won't be able to hold the line. Then there's MI5; they are chasing their tails trying to keep a lid on the bloody Muslims and failing. What they don't know is that we are working on the Muslims to wind them up to cause trouble when we need it. The government won't know which way to turn."

"Why the hell would the Muslims work with us?"

"Those thick shits have no idea they are working for us. As far as I can see they're terminally stupid anyway. They come to Europe to escape from bloody awful regimes and then demand that Europe changes to be like the dump they've just escaped from. How thick is that, I ask you?"

Billy realised his mouth was hanging open and snapped it shut. "So what's our part in this master plot supposed to be?"

"Sympathy mostly. The Americans have this thing about longing for their original homeland. They get all misty-eyed about the 'auld country' and it's up to us to stoke that fire. We get them wound up to give us money and we use that to bring our weapon stocks up to the levels we need in time for the final armed insurrection."

"Won't they be wary of funding terrorists after 9/11?"

"You'd think so, but no. Anyway, we aren't terrorists; we're freedom fighters trying to throw off the oppressive yoke of the British. We tell the Yanks that the money goes to support the widows and orphans or to pay for hospital treatment for the victims of British torture."

"All the while using the National Health Service and drawing the unemployment benefits from the state? Anyhow, what torture and what oppression?"

"The torture we tell them about. You sing the songs and I'll tell the stories we want them to hear. You just nod sadly in the background when I'm doing that."

"Are you sure this is going to work?"

"Sure as eggs is eggs, Billy. That's why you play that tired old guitar of your da's. We tell them how he was murdered by the British Special Forces and had that slogan carved into his back. With your dark hair and blue eyes you look the part of the sad, put-upon Irish patriot. You are going to be the embodiment of The Minstrel Boy and we'll have them eating this stuff up."

Chapter 4

Flaherty got them a yellow cab outside the airport and they drove into Manhattan. The city looked just the way it was supposed to in Billy's imagination, fuelled as it was by a hundred movies. He saw the road signs that told him the streets he was driving down, that he had never dared hope to see, yet here he was.

The cab pulled up outside a nondescript brown apartment building and Flaherty paid. Billy stood on the sidewalk and looked around him at the people bustling by. They all seemed to be in a terrible hurry to get somewhere important. At the glass door of the apartment block Flaherty pressed a button among a mass of others and a voice asked what they wanted.

"'Tis the business of 'Ourselves Alone' now."

The door buzzed and Flaherty pushed it open and held it for Billy with his bag and guitar case to struggle through. They took the elevator to the tenth floor and as the doors slid open they found themselves looking at a plump man with the over rosy cheeks of the overweight.

"So it's yerself, Flaherty. It's been a long time. Come away and bring yer singing monkey with you."

The plump one turned and led them along a dingy corridor to a door that stood open on the left-hand side. Once inside Billy dropped his luggage and looked about. The apartment was neat, but sparsely furnished. The few pictures on the wall had obviously come from a cheap shop somewhere and gave no clue about the occupant.

"The spare bedroom is down that way and there's an extra mattress on the floor for you."

"What about your wife?" Flaherty asked.

"She's away to stay with her mother upstate. She'll not be coming back till you're long gone. So there's no chance of her saying anything out of turn later."

Flaherty pointed at the plump one. "I should introduce you. This one's O'Connell, a man the British would dearly love to have their hands on. He may not look it now, but he was a terror to the British back in the old days. He was a friend of yer da as well."

O'Connell looked at Billy keenly. "So who's his da then?"

"This is Seamus Murphy's boy. Name of Billy. He's going to be our Minstrel when we hit the Irish bars."

"Billy, is it? I did know yer da. Didn't know he had kids, though. Him and me pulled some fine strokes together. I was sorry to hear the British hit squad got him. The way I heard it, they gave him a hard time before they shot him."

Billy nodded. "He didn't go easy or quickly, that's for sure. He was a right mess when the police found him."

"And now you're joining the family business, eh?"

"Seems that way. When do we start?"

O'Connell shook his head and smiled. "Ah, the eagerness of the young. Well, I've got you a booking at a bar a couple of blocks over. Popular place it is, and the owner is a supporter. He's been passing the word that you're coming, so we should get a good turnout."

Billy nodded. "And what are they expecting me to sing?"

O'Connell nodded towards Flaherty. "That's his part of the business now. Me, I'm just here to get you the bookings. I've got a list here somewhere of the Irish pubs you're performing in all over New York."

Flaherty leaned back into the cushions of the cheap sofa. "Well now, I've been thinking about it. I think we'll start with 'The Minstrel Boy'. I want that to become your signature tune at the start of each performance. Then we run through a few of the rebel songs that everyone knows. Get them singing along so they feel the Irish in the blood. We'll take a break in the middle where I might give them a few stories of the struggle. I'll be laying the British atrocities on with a trowel, so make sure you look sad and nod in the right places. By the time the break is over they should be well into the beer so you start tugging at the heartstrings. 'The Fields of Athenry' is a great tear-jerker."

Billy nodded slowly. "I can do all that with no problem. Anything else?"

"Indeed yes. Not sure if this will work, but if we get them drinking Guinness and Irish whiskey they'll be more susceptible. They're not used to decent beer since most of them will drink this American piss water. Try working in that Monty

Python joke about sex in a canoe. That way when we start to ask for donations they'll be reaching deeper."

Billy looked between the two older men. "Are you sure these people are this dumb? Are they really going to fall for all this guff?"

O'Connell laughed quietly. "They're not dumb, lad, but they are naïve. They have this rosy view of the old country. They think they're as Irish as the morning mist, though most of them have never been near the place. That's what we're playing on. It worked before and it will work again, never fear."

Chapter 5

The bar was better than any of the pubs back in Belfast that Billy was used to. The Irish tricolour hung behind the stage and there were paintings and photographs around the walls of all things Irish. Hell, there was even a harp fixed on the wall behind the bar. They had spoken with the barman before they started to set up for the performance, and Billy had been hard pressed not to laugh at the strange version of an Irish accent the man spouted at them.

He set the old guitar down at the back of the raised platform and adjusted the microphone. The spotlight dazzled him and he had it turned down so he could see the audience and try to relate to them. He didn't like the chair they had put out for him, so he took one of the bar stools and moved it across the room. If nothing else, it would reduce the number of people drinking with their backs to him.

He strummed the guitar and then deliberately slackened one string so it was out of tune. The barman brought him the glass of water he had asked for and he was ready. He walked across and sat down with Flaherty and O'Connell.

"All set now, Billy?"

"All set, Paddy. Are we sure the people are going to come tonight? I don't want to sing to an empty room on my first gig in America."

O'Connell put his beer down. "They'll be here, Billy boy. It's a working day, remember, and the people we want have jobs to go to. They'll call in here to get their dinner and to listen to you. The Yanks eat early most of the time. They'll be gulping down the black pudding and colcannon, and pretending they like it, anytime now. The barman tells me they've even got coddle and soda bread on the go back there. Not a burger in the place tonight."

"So what do we do while we're waiting?"

"You could have a pint or two to loosen your throat, Billy."

Billy shook his head. "Not for me. I don't like to drink when I'm singing. Doesn't work for me. How about you tell me about the strokes you pulled with me da? Are you not worried the British will send someone after you one of these days?"

O'Connell leaned back and laughed. "Oh, the British would love to have a word with me, no doubt of that, but they don't know where I am and they aren't sure it was me with your da."

"So what did you do that was so special?"

"Can I tell him, Patrick? Are we sure he's one of us?"

Flaherty gave them both a slow smile. "It's in the blood, Michael. It's natural he would want to know about what his da did in the Troubles. Tell him about the La Mon. That was quite a stroke, even if it went a bit wrong."

"What's La Mon then?"

"Ah, Billy boy, La Mon was a fancy restaurant in County Down and we showed them what the IRA could do that night, even though it was a bit of a cock-up."

Chapter 6
17th February 1978

"It was a cold night even for February, I remember, a real lazy wind blowing across the car park outside the restaurant."

"Lazy wind?" Billy asked.

"Too lazy to go round, it cuts right through you." O'Connell smiled. "Anyway it was bloody freezing. Bobby Murphy, no relative I guess, was there to set the bomb and me and your da were along to help him. He took the bomb and hung it outside the window on meat hooks. We carried the four containers of petrol across the park and put them around the bomb on the windowsill and hanging off more hooks. It wasn't ordinary petrol, though. We'd put a load of sugar in it to make a poor man's napalm."

"Why would you put sugar in it?"

O'Connell chuckled. "Well you see, Billy boy, the sugar makes it stick to whatever it splashes on and makes it burn more. Anyway, we set the bomb and the jellied petrol and we were backing off to watch the fun when Bobby says he has to go and phone in a warning. It was the way we did things back then."

"But me and your da didn't agree. We thought the RUC were inside having a meeting so we wanted them there when the bomb went off. Bobby insisted we had to do it right. What he didn't know was that me and your da had been in the phone box and cut the handset off on our way in. This was back in the days before mobile phones, you see. Anyhow, Bobby couldn't phone from there, so he set off to get to the next phone box down the road. We stayed to watch the fun."

"Bobby drove away and, wouldn't you know, he ran into an army checkpoint on the way. That slowed him down a lot, so when he got to the phone there was only a few minutes before the bomb was due to go. He got the warning in all right, but when the police called the restaurant to tell them it had already blown up."

"Me and your da had gone into the trees at the back of the car park to watch. We made damn sure we were well away from the blast area, I can tell you. So the bomb went off right on time and the petrol blew. My God, but it was a hell of a sight. A huge brilliant fireball blew out into the night. We could see all the countryside around us. And the fireball went in through the window as well: my but those people could scream. The crowd came pouring out of the doors in a mad panic. Some of them had their clothes on fire and one woman was running and screaming with her hair burning. She had to be rugby tackled to the ground before they could put her out."

O'Connell took a long sip of his beer. "It was only a minute or so before the roof of the place was ablaze. A real intense fire, it was, and it wasn't long before rafters gave way and it all caved in. Hell, it was good to watch.

"Then the police and fire trucks arrived with their sirens screaming so we took a hike to get the hell out of there. Not a minute too soon either. The army arrived and threw a cordon around the scene, but we were far enough away by then and they never knew we were there. Bobby Murphy got picked up, though, and they gave him twelve life sentences for manslaughter. It would have been murder if he hadn't called the warning in. Bobby was a good lad, though, and he never said a word about us helping him. They let him out of jail in 1995."

"You said it was a cock-up. Why was that?"

O'Connell chuckled. "Turns out the RUC meeting that we wanted to hit was the week before. The people inside were from the Irish Collie Club and the Northern Ireland Junior Motor Cycle Club. Both lots were having their annual dinner dances. They had only just had the first course when it all went off, so they didn't get their money's worth, eh."

"How many people were hurt?"

"Hurt? Oh no, Billy boy. We killed twelve of them. Burned to a crisp they were; took a long time to identify them. The doctors said they looked like charred logs of wood. About another thirty had serious burns that they won't forget, ever. The RUC passed out leaflets with gruesome photos on to try and motivate people to tell what they knew. I've still got one in my scrapbook if you want to see it?"

Billy sat in silence looking at O'Connell, who was enjoying his recollections.

"And now you see, Billy, why the British would like a word with me if they knew where I was. That's why it's not a good idea for me to go home anytime soon, but I can still help the cause from here."

Chapter 7

Billy took his place on the stool and looked out at the crowd. As promised, the room had filled and the audience watched him expectantly.

He fiddled with the guitar to correct the tuning he had altered earlier. "Sure, I don't know what happened. This damn thing was in tune when I bought it."

He got the laugh he expected and smiled at the audience. "A thing I never expected in an Irish bar is to see Irishmen drinking American beer instead of porter. A friend of mine told me that drinking American beer is like having sex in a canoe." He paused. "It's fucking close to water."

The laugh was bigger this time and he saw people nudging each other. He plucked the opening bars of the tune out of his guitar and then launched into 'The Minstrel Boy' as Flaherty had told him. He could see that the audience was with him by the end of the first verse and they were tapping the table in time with his singing. This should be a good night.

Even the drunks at the bar had turned around and were singing along by the time he finished his third song. He went for 'The Rising of The Moon' and he knew he had them eating out of his hand by the way they belted out the chorus. He had never had reactions like this back in Belfast, but then he supposed he was more of a novelty here in New York. He finished the first set and as he walked through the tables to sit with Flaherty and O'Connell he was slapped on the back by people who were now forcing the unfamiliar dark brew down their necks.

As he sat, a plate of boiled bacon and cabbage was put in front of him. He looked at Flaherty quizzically.

"Eat it up, boy. It's the food of our misted homeland and these daft buggers need to see just how Irish we are. I'm going to do a little talking before you sing again. I'll tell them of the glorious cause and then you sing the tear-jerkers. They'll be fighting to fill the bucket with cash by the end of the evening."

Flaherty was as good as his word and spoon-fed the audience with imaginary tales of woe from the 'Emerald Isle'. Billy sat quietly behind him and watched. They were lapping it up. Could they really be this naïve? Apparently the answer was yes. The strong beer, the songs and the longing for a fabled homeland had worked the magic.

He tried to stay composed as Flaherty told the story of his da, Seamus Murphy, being found face down in the alley with an anti-IRA slogan carved into his naked back. He told how they had found the AVNI calling card stuffed into his mouth. The cries of horror when he explained that AVNI was a mystery group. Nobody knew who they were, Flaherty explained, but the IRA suspected it was ex-Special Forces troops who had not accepted the peace accords.

Then it was time for Billy to sing again. He sang the old songs of longing and heartache. He gave them 'Kevin Barry' and he could see they were affected by the story. Then it was time to

31

finish and he gave them 'The Fields of Athenry'. In the reflected light he could see that some of them were weeping and many were holding hands across the tables.

He finished the song and sat quietly as the spotlight turned off and O'Connell and Flaherty walked through the crowd passing the collection buckets. So many of them came to the edge of the stage and shook his hand, it was almost overwhelming. He wished his ma and Niamh had been here to see this. Maybe then they'd realise he wasn't a waste of space.

The crowd thinned out and a short while later the bar closed. He sat with the two older men as they counted their takings.

"We did well, Billy boy. You're good at this. Another week or two in New York working our way through the Irish bars that Michael has booked us into should see us well set up."

Billy sipped at his first beer of the evening. "But is this enough to fund the cause back home?"

Flaherty glanced at O'Connell before he spoke. "Son, this is just the cover story for the authorities. The serious money comes from other people we talk to on the quiet. There's businessmen know that there is good money to be made out of the confusion of creating a new country. They will be giving us the big money and we'll use that to buy the supplies we need to make this thing happen."

Chapter 8

He walked into the apartment kitchen, rubbing his eyes, to get a coffee. Flaherty was already there and the pot was boiling. Billy eyed the bacon that was frying in the pan and decided against it this morning.

"Go and give O'Connell a shout, will you, Billy? He likes his coffee fresh."

Billy shrugged and walked back along the short corridor. He knocked on the bedroom door, but got no answer, so he turned the handle and walked in. The bed had not been slept in by the look of it, so he returned to the kitchen.

"He's no here. Looks like he got up early or maybe he's sleeping it off in the drunk tank somewhere."

Flaherty nodded as he dished up the bacon. "He was hitting the whiskey hard last night. Did you see him come back here?"

"No, I walked home with you, if you remember. You weren't too steady either."

Flaherty smiled. "And I'm paying for it this morning. Not sure these American headache tablets are doing anything for me. I guess they are made for the hangovers you get from American piss-water beer."

"I dunno, I quite like it. Doesn't give me a bad stomach like the Guinness."

"Don't you say that during a performance, Billy lad. You're supposed to be as Irish as the Blarney Stone, so y'are."

"Give me credit, Paddy. I didn't laugh when you started laying on the 'begorahs' and 'bejasuses' last night, did I?"

"Ye think that was a bit much? They were lapping it up. They could smell the peat fires in the wee bothies out beyond the bog. Feckin eejits."

Billy chuckled. "So what's the plan today? It's our last night in New York, so do we get to go and see some of the tourist stuff before we go?"

Flaherty took a forkful of bacon and spoke as he chewed. "You can if you want. O'Connell is taking me to see a guy who can do us a bit of good." He checked his watch. "If he doesn't get back soon we're going to be late for the meeting and that's not good."

"So what do we do?"

Flaherty looked up at the loud rap on the door. "Go answer that, Billy."

Billy put down his coffee and walked to the apartment door. He looked through the security eyehole and was startled to see a large black New York policeman standing outside. He opened the door.

"Good morning, officer. Can I help?"

The officer looked past him and then down at Billy. "Is this Michael O'Connell's apartment?"

"It is. I'm staying here on holiday, but you'll need to come back later. He hasn't come home yet. He got a bit drunk last night, you see."

"He got more than drunk. He got dead. We've just found his body in the alley out back."

"Oh Christ! Was it a robbery?"

"He's still got his wallet and watch, so maybe not. That's how we found his address. You know him well enough to identify the body?"

Billy nodded. "I'll get my jacket and be right with you."

He walked through into the living room and picked up the jacket he had tossed across the back of a chair.

"Michael's dead," he hissed to Flaherty. "The police have found his body. I'm going down to identify it."

"Don't get involved, for fuck's sake."

Billy shook his head. "I have to. It'll look bloody strange if the people in his apartment don't try to help, won't it?"

"Ah yes, true enough. Try not to give them much information, though."

"I know the score. I've lived in Belfast all my life, remember."

With his jacket on he walked out of the apartment and closed the door behind him. He walked to the elevator with the policeman and they rode to the ground floor in silence. Out in the filthy alley behind the apartment block there were three NYPD cruisers and the Medical Examiner's truck. Billy was taken across to where the overflowing dumpsters stood and, as he approached, he could see a pair of legs on top of the garbage.

He walked around behind the bin and looked down at the body that lay there. The shirt and jacket had been ripped off and the words 'IRA Scum' had been carved into his back.

"Can you turn him over?"

The police officer looked to the Medical Examiner for permission, and when he nodded took hold of the corpse's shoulder and turned him. As he rolled O'Connell's head fell back, far too far. The deep slash across his throat gaped open and Billy gagged.

"Sorry about that, sir. I should have warned you. Does it look like your friend?"

Billy leaned forward and looked at the face. He nodded and stepped back.

"That's Michael O'Connell, for sure."

The Medical Examiner held out a card for Billy to see. "Does this mean anything to you?"

Billy looked at the white pasteboard. The crossed rifles and the red hand of Ulster were clear despite the blood stain, as were the letters AVNI.

"Sorry, sir. No idea what that might be. Is it significant?"

"It was stuck between the victim's teeth. Some kind of sick calling card. Does the 'IRA SCUM' on his back mean anything to you?"

"Michael was Irish, sir, but I don't know that he had anything to do with the IRA. Maybe they got the wrong guy?"

"Maybe. That's for the homicide detectives to find out. Thanks for your help."

Back in the apartment Billy dropped his jacket on the floor and went to vomit into the kitchen sink. Flaherty watched him from the living room. He let him finish before he spoke.

"Bad, was it?"

Billy nodded. "They nearly cut his damned head off, they slashed his throat so deep. It's bad,

Paddy. They carved IRA SCUM into his back and they shoved another of those AVNI cards in his mouth."

"Just like your da?"

"Just like that, yeah."

Chapter 9

"What do we do if the police want to talk to me again?"

"Nothing. Did you give them our forwarding address?"

"I don't know where we're going, so how could I?"

Flaherty grinned. "And now you know why I only tell you what you need to know. Finish packing your bag. We've got a plane to catch."

"So where are we going then?"

"Boston. We've got a friend there who will pick us up at Logan and give us a place to sleep."

"Another one like O'Connell?"

"If you mean is he a retired IRA volunteer, then yes, and that means we can trust him. He's agreed to find us gigs and to make sure we are looked after."

"I meant is he another one hiding out in America to avoid being arrested at home?"

Flaherty paused in his packing and looked at Billy calmly. "Is that a problem for some reason?"

"No, not really. I just want to know who I'm dealing with."

"OK, listen. During the Troubles some of us did some pretty extreme things. They were effective and forced the British to negotiate. But they don't forget and it seems they don't forgive. Some of the boys knew they would be hunted down, so they got the hell out of it. They are scattered all over the place, which fits in nicely for us. They know that, when we finally win, they can come home again and live out their lives in peace."

"And that's why they work for us?"

"Work with us, Billy. You have to remember that when we unite Ireland it will be a true socialist republic. We are working for equality, which is why so many of those lefty British politicians help us out. Useful idiots, as Marx said."

"I don't care about the politics. I'll tell you for free this trip is to get me noticed and maybe get me a record deal."

Flaherty smiled and closed his case. "No problem with that, son. You do your part and I'll see what our contacts can do to help you get what you want as well. How's that for a fair deal?"

Billy zipped his heavy shoulder bag. "Sounds good to me. So let's go sing in Boston then. You got some more of these rich business people to see there?"

"See now, Billy, that's not your part of this deal. Better you just forget about that and concentrate on the singing and telling your couple of jokes."

The Jet Blue flight left JFK right on time at five minutes before eleven. An hour later they touched down again at Boston Logan airport and by half past midnight they had their bags and were walking out of the terminal building.

Flaherty stopped on the sidewalk and looked around him. "He should be here somewhere, the old beggar."

"Flaherty! Long time no see."

Billy spun round to see a short man with a bushy white beard and a broad smile walking towards them with his hand out in greeting. Flaherty stepped forward and gripped his hand.

"Driscoll, you old poacher. What are you hiding behind that fur hedgerow for?"

"I could tell you it's all part of my cunning disguise, but in truth I've got a skin complaint and it hurts like hell to shave, so I gave up. And how's yerself? Still got your hair, I see, though it seems to have been snowing up there."

"Ach, we can catch the years up later, Peter. Now you need to meet my Minstrel. This is Billy Murphy. You remember Seamus Murphy? Well, this is his boy, or at least, one of them."

Billy reached out and shook the man's hand. "Billy, is it? Welcome to Boston. I've got a few busy days planned out for you. There's a load of Irish bars just gagging to have you on stage, to give them a taste of the auld sod. For now let's get you into the car and out of the cold. Don't want you losing your voice, now, do we?"

They walked to the car park and loaded the bags into the trunk then climbed inside. Driscoll drove them into the Ted Williams tunnel, talking all the while about his adopted city.

"This was all done in what they called the Big Dig. Tunnelled under the city for years, so they did, but look at it now. Wonderful piece of engineering. Very welcome when the snow comes, it is."

"Does it snow here much, Mr Driscoll?"

"Snow? Oh hell yes. We get some serious big drifts. There's so much that when it melts and runs into the harbour it kills some of the salt water fish and that's no lie. And anyway, call me Peter since we're all to be friends and comrades."

They pulled up outside a neat row house in a quiet side street and Driscoll waved his hand towards it. "*Mi casa es su casa*. Well, at least for two weeks it is. I've sent the wife away down to Florida to visit her mother, just as I was told to. She was delighted to go; she doesn't much like the cold. I think we'll be retiring down there when the time comes."

"You don't want to retire to Ireland?"

"Have you been to Florida, son? No? Well, let me tell you, it's warm all the time and they have more golf courses than you'd believe. I've got a place picked out near Melbourne on the Indian River, where the fish just beg to be caught and I can moor my boat."

"You've got a boat?"

"Not yet, but I will have after this job. The boys have promised me a nice gratuity if it all goes well, and it will. I have it all set up, including the specials for you, Paddy."

Chapter 10

Driscoll came down the stairs to see why the TV was still on. "Can't sleep, young Billy?"

"No, Mr Driscoll er, Peter, I had some things to think about."

"Such as?"

Billy switched the TV off with the remote. "It just seems strange all these retired IRA men being over here and nobody looking for them."

Driscoll sat down opposite Billy. "It's not quite like that, you see. We aren't really retired, it's just that Ireland got too hot for us. If we let the British catch us then the propaganda goes their way and an awful lot of this struggle is about the way things look to the civilians. So it's best we stay out of the way and let younger lads like yerself take the lead for a while."

"O'Connell told me about how him and me da firebombed the La Mon Restaurant and that's why he was hiding out in New York."

Driscoll grinned. "O'Connell did way more than that, son. That one was his favourite story right enough, but the British wanted him for a few jobs he pulled. I think he thought that was one of the high points of the campaign."

"So what else had he done for the cause?"

"If we're to stay up telling old yarns I think I need a good strong brew. You want a mug of tea?"

Billy nodded. "I could go for a tea. You want me to make it?"

"No, I'll do it. Don't want you blundering around the kitchen this time of night. The wife would be all upset if things aren't where she left them. Very particular, she is. I tell her it's OCD, but she's just a really neat person."

Billy stayed in his chair looking out at the moonlit street while Driscoll busied himself in the kitchen. He came back carrying a tray with two steaming mugs of tea and a plate of unfamiliar biscuits.

"Here you go, Billy, try some of these. The Yanks call them cookies, but they're good. A lot of the American convenience food is good. Full of sugar and salt, of course, but tastes great."

Billy nibbled a biscuit and leaned back with his tea cradled between his hands. "So you were going to tell me about O'Connell and his adventures. Then what about yourself? You must have a reason for being here?"

"I do, I really do. I tell you what, though, instead of me telling you all the tales in one night I'll be like Scheherazade and tell you my yarns one at a time."

"Scheherazade?"

Driscoll sighed. "The storyteller in *One Thousand and One Nights*. Don't they teach you anything in school these days?"

Billy gave a weak smile. "They probably do, but school was never really my thing. Except the football and the Gaelic. I liked them well enough."

Driscoll shook his head sadly. "Well, you're not alone in being let down by schools in Ireland. I suppose there was a lot of distraction in the Troubles as well."

He took a long pull at his tea and then looked up at the ceiling. "So which of the O'Connell exploits shall I tell you tonight then?"

"What are my choices?" Billy asked as he put his mug back down on the low table.

"Let's see. There's Bloody Sunday or the Mountbatten boat killing. Then again, I think he also did the Manchester bombing."

"I've heard of Bloody Sunday, so what about that one?"

"Ah no. I'll tell you about the coach on the M62 first. That was a strange one."

Chapter 11
4th February 1974

Driscoll leaned back in his chair and sipped his tea. "So back in the seventies squaddies weren't paid much, so most of them couldn't afford cars. Most of them were stationed a long way from where they joined up and where their families lived. So the army had a system of coaches that gave them the chance to get home for the weekend. They'd catch the coach, on the Friday, in their barracks that went to a central place and then change to the coach that was going where they wanted to be. On the Sunday it all went into reverse. Good little system, but they hadn't counted on us. They thought they were safe on the mainland.

"So O'Connell got himself a car and followed the coaches for a couple of weeks to work out the system. Once he knew where he was going he got one of the active service units in England to supply him with a bomb on a timer.

"The coach was filling up in the Manchester bus station and the luggage door was standing open. The squaddies just walked up and flung their bags in, then got on the coach. O'Connell waited for a gap and then strolled up and put his bag inside and walked as if he was going to get on board. As he got near the door he made a big show of patting his pockets as if he had forgotten something. He walked away to the little shop that was in the bus station, but of course he never came back.

"So right on time the coach pulled out and set off for wherever it was going. O'Connell followed in the car. He always liked to watch his handiwork. It was just after midnight when they passed junction twenty-six and the bomb went off. Twenty-five pounds of high explosive in the luggage locker below the coach does a lot of damage. The police were picking body parts up from two hundred and fifty yards away the next morning."

Billy picked up his tea and took a swig; it was cold by now, but he barely noticed. "So how many people did it kill?"

"There was eleven dead and more than fifty injured. One more died four days later in hospital. Nine of the ones killed outright were soldiers, the other three were civilians. One of the silly bastards had his family along with him."

"Family?"

"Aye. His wife and two kids. Two boys, five and two years old. There was a six-year- old as well that got badly burned. A good mission that was. O'Connell was away and clear down the motorway before the body parts had finished dropping out of the sky."

Billy shuddered at the image conjured in his mind's eye. "You said it was a strange one."

Driscoll nodded. "I did, and so it was. The press and the politicians went crazy demanding that swift justice be meted out to the madman who had perpetrated such a horrendous crime. Their words, not mine. Anyhow, that put the police under a hell of a lot of pressure, so it was a gift from heaven when a woman came forward and confessed to planting the bomb. She also confessed to the bombing of Euston Railway Station in London and the attack on the Latimer Military College."

"But I thought you said O'Connell did it?"

"He did. Turns out this poor soul had mental health problems. There was no evidence against her, just her rambling confession, but that was enough for the police and the courts. They locked her up and threw away the key. Hell, we even wrote to them and told them she was nothing to do with it and that it had been done by one of our Active Service Units. They didn't want to know. She stayed in jail until 1992 when the appeal court ruled it had been a 'grave miscarriage of justice'. The poor soul was just some more collateral damage, as the Americans call it."

"And nobody connected O'Connell to it?"

"Not till years later when some traitor put his name in the frame to try and get a lighter sentence. But by then they were more wary and there was still no real evidence apart from the word of an informer. This was in the days before there was so much CCTV, you see, or they might have film of him planting it."

"Sounds pretty grim, Peter. Did it never bother O'Connell?"

"He never lost a moment's sleep over it."

"Not even the kids?"

"Not even the kids. Now you need some sleep. You're performing tomorrow and we need you on top form."

Chapter 12

Billy looked around the performing room above the main bar. This was really something. It knocked the pubs in Belfast into a cocked hat. The barman and the owner had been welcoming without any of the phoney Irish accents that he had run into in New York. He played a few chords and Flaherty standing at the end of the room nodded; the acoustics were as good as the venue.

Flaherty walked between the tables. "Have you decided what you're singing tonight?"

"I have, Paddy. I thought I'd stay with much the same format as we used in the Big Apple, but I'm going to try another couple of songs that don't get heard too often."

"You sure about that?"

"Sure enough. Once I've got them warmed up I'll introduce the new ones. If I'm right we'll have them roaring the chorus. Then after the break I'll slow it down again and sing them some of the tear-jerkers."

"You make sure you finish on 'The Fields of Athenry', though. That one had them weeping into their beer a couple of times."

"Are we expecting much of a turnout here in Boston?"

Flaherty snorted. "You wait and see, Billy boy. There's a lot of Irish in this town. We got the bulk of our American funding from here in the seventies and eighties with Noraid. I'll lay you good money it'll be standing room only by the end of the night. Driscoll has been putting the word round for weeks, so he has."

"Working hard to get his boat then."

"Boat? Oh I think that was his little joke. I don't think he'd risk a boat after the Mountbatten incident. The British would love to return that favour."

"Mountbatten? Where's that?"

"Do they teach you no history at all in schools? It not a where, it's a who and I won't steal Driscoll's thunder. Let him tell you the tale."

Billy shrugged and turned back to adjust the microphone and the stool. "Can we turn that damned light down a bit? The Yanks seem to like things way too bright. I want to make it feel cosy in here for the punters."

Flaherty laughed. "My, aren't we becoming the diva!"

Billy stopped and gazed at Flaherty for a moment. "No, I'm not. You want this performance to have an impact on the audience and I'm learning what I can do. If we get the atmosphere right then they'll enjoy it even more and I'll have them feeling it by the end of the night."

Flaherty paused. "Sorry, Billy. You're quite right. I'll get the light adjusted for you." He looked at Billy for a long moment. "You really are getting the hang of this now, aren't you?"

"I think I am. These people react to the songs and I can feel them getting it when I sing. It's never been like that before in the pubs back home."

They both looked across the room as Driscoll clumped up the stairs and appeared at the side of the small bar. "You two nearly ready? The bar downstairs is filling up and they are getting restless to get up here."

Flaherty nodded at Billy, who nodded back. "Fling wide the doors! Bring in the adoring masses to hear the songs of the auld sod."

Driscoll shook his head and grinned. "Or I could just tell them we're ready for them, eh?"

Moments later the flood of people from the downstairs bar poured into the performing room. Billy watched as they found tables and settled down with their drinks in their hands. He stepped up onto the small stage and looked around at the sea of faces looking back at him expectantly. His eyes drifted down to the table right in front of the stage where the four girls sat. The one directly opposite him gave him a smile that made his heart lurch. He smiled back, then pulled himself together and sat on the stool.

He fumbled with the tuning before he dropped his opening joke into the silence. "Sure I don't know what happened here. It was in tune when I bought it."

He got the small laugh he was hoping for and strummed the strings quietly. He looked down at the girl again and decided against the canoe joke. He didn't want her to think he was crude. His fingers found the strings and the opening notes of 'The Minstrel Boy' floated across the room. He ran through the tunes just as he had planned and he heard the audience singing along with him. Time

51

for one of the new ones, he thought, so he gave them 'Come Out Ye Black and Tans'. They loved it and were roaring the chorus with him. He looked across the crowd at Flaherty and saw him nod.

The first set ended and he stepped down to a remarkably loud round of applause. He was about to walk through the crowd when he found himself facing the girl and looking into the bluest eyes he had ever seen.

"Hello …?" He made it a question.I'm Billy. Did you like the songs?"

"Kathleen … and yes, I think you have a wonderful voice."

"Can I buy you a drink, Kathleen?"

She shook her head and he saw her long auburn hair catch the light. "It's OK, my friend Janet is getting me one."

"Sure and that's a shame. I was hoping to have an excuse to talk to you some more."

She smiled that wonderful smile. "You could buy me one when you've finished singing then."

He smiled back. "I'll hold you to that and I'll sing one song just for you. Do you have the Gaelic?"

"I don't."

"Then I can tell you what it means afterwards."

Her friend Janet came back with the tray of drinks and set them on the table. She looked at the two of them and grinned. The other two girls at the table smiled and nudged each other, but Billy didn't mind at all. He touched Kathleen's hand and then walked away to where Flaherty and Driscoll sat at a table in the rear corner of the room.

"That's a fine looking colleen you were talking to there, Billy," Driscoll said as he handed him his glass of water.

"She's beautiful. Her name's Kathleen. I'm going to sing her a special song."

"'I'll take you home again, Kathleen', perhaps?"

Billy shook his head. "Nothing so obvious. She's worth more than that."

Flaherty glanced across the room at the girls' table. "Don't you start getting distracted now. We're here to do a job, not run your love life."

Billy set his glass down carefully. "I'll sing your songs and I'll pluck their Irish heartstrings for you, but you don't own me, Paddy, and that girl is something special to look at."

Flaherty grunted, but said no more. As the audience came back to their tables from the bar he walked to the stage and started his stories of British oppression. Most of the people on the room turned their heads and looked at Billy as Flaherty told the story of Seamus Murphy being found face down in a dirty alley, with the signs of torture cut into his flesh.

Billy stood and walked back to the stage through the silent audience. He sat and gave them the 'My Last Farewell' and he knew he had them in the palm of his hand. He sang the old sad songs of longing and loss, and then he paused and looked down at Kathleen. He stood up from the stool and leaned his guitar against the wall. Then he stepped silently back to the microphone and raised it up so he could sing standing. He paused, and then he raised his voice to give them '*Mo Ghille Mear*'. Halfway through the song he dropped his eyes to Kathleen and never looked away until he reached the end of the song.

The applause was rapturous as he picked the guitar up again and sat on the stool. He doubted if any of the Americans had understood a word of the Gaelic, but they had felt the sound of Ireland deep within them, or maybe that had been the drink.

His last song as usual was 'The Fields of Athenry' and as usual he saw the tears start to appear here and there in the room. The hands stretched across the tables and gripped each other and he saw them sway with the sad chords of the old tear-jerker. As he finished there was a silence and then the applause started as they rose to their feet and yelled their approval. This never happened in Belfast.

He stepped down from the stage and looked for Kathleen. She was sitting quietly at the table and her friends were making a rapid exit to leave them alone.

He sat down and she smiled at him. "That was beautiful. What does it mean?"

"*Mo Ghille Mear*, it means My Gallant Hero. Shall I tell you all the words?"

She shook her head. "Another time maybe. For now, I want you to tell me about Billy Murphy."

He reached out and took her hand across the table. "Now that will be a boring story. I'd much rather hear about the beautiful Kathleen from Boston."

Chapter 13

"You're late back, Billy."

Billy flopped in a chair by the empty fireplace. "I was walking Kathleen back home."

"You walked through the city at this time of night?"

Billy nodded. "Sure and why not? It's not too cold and it's a clear night."

"Well, I hope Kathleen told you which areas to avoid. It can be risky if you don't know your way round."

"Peter, I'm from Belfast. I grew up in the Troubles. I'm a child of a bloody civil war. This is a nice town. I think you've been out of Ireland too long."

"Well, you're not wrong about it being a nice town. Now, despite your love life getting in the way, I've got you a magic venue for tonight. We've got The Black Rose on State Street."

"Is that something special?"

"Are you kidding? It's the Black Rose. It's only the best Irish bar in the city and they have live music there every night. It's the place everybody dreams of playing and you've got a solo spot tomorrow night."

"How did you pull that off, if it's so special?"

Driscoll shook his head. "Trust me, it's special. If you do a good show in there you're going to get noticed. The word will get round to all the other Irish bars. They'll be beating a path to our door trying to book you. Tell you what, we'll go down there for lunch tomorrow and you can take a look at it. It's all dark polished wood and right on a corner so they'll hear you out in the street. Brilliant place."

"I get the picture. The Black Rose is a good venue for us."

"The best, bar none."

"I'll see you in the morning then," Billy said as he heaved himself out of his chair and headed for the stairs.

***

"So? Did I lie?"

Billy stood in the Black Rose bar and slowly turned around, taking it all in. "You didn't lie. This is a damned nice place right enough."

"I've been passing the word all morning. With the usual customers plus the ones we bring in this place will be packed to the rafters tonight and these people appreciate Irish music. This is going to be a hard one to beat, Billy boy."

"Can you reserve a table right by the stage? I want to invite Kathleen along. She'll probably bring her friends as well."

"Not sure that's a good idea, Billy. Flaherty wasn't too keen on you getting distracted, you know."

Billy sighed. "He wants a show, I'll give him a show. It'll be the best he's seen. I want Kathleen to see me at my best."

Driscoll shrugged and then nodded. "OK, Billy, I'll get you a reserved table right next to where you sing, but I tell you, Flaherty won't like it."

Billy grinned. "I'll bet you $100 that Flaherty likes it fine well by the end of the evening."

"Have you got $100?"

"No, but I will have when you have to pay up tonight."

Driscoll laughed. "Well, we'll see. Now, though, I'm going to give you some material for the show. You see, Boston is special for us in more than one way. The American Revolution started here for real with the tea being thrown into the harbour. Then later on when the British had been kicked out the last troops embarked at the Long Wharf."

"Where's the Long Wharf then?"

"If you step outside that door over there and turn left, you walk along State Street and you come to the Long Wharf. There's a big Marriott Hotel there now, but once it was the scene of a piece of history we want to repeat. That's where the British army finally shipped out of America." Driscoll looked at his watch. "Do you like fish?"

"What? Well, yes, I like fish. What's that got to do with anything?"

"We're going to walk down to the Long Wharf and just by the quay is the best fish restaurant you are ever going to find. 'Legal Sea Food' is just there and it's great. Come on, I'm buying and then you can tell me why Flaherty is going to like Kathleen."

Chapter 14
27th August 1979

They came out of the front door of Legal Sea Foods and walked along the front of the Marriott, up the Long Wharf beside the whale-watching boats. "Did I lie about the seafood then, Billy?"

Billy shook his head. "You did not. That was quite something. So where are we going?"

Driscoll pointed to an outdoor seating area alongside the whale boats. "Just here. I thought this would be a good time to continue your education about the Troubles. To understand it all, you really need to know what we did to drive the British to the negotiating table."

They sat and Driscoll ordered coffee for them both. While they waited Billy leafed through the small brochure about the whales that could be seen just outside Boston on the Stellwagen Bank.

"D'ye think Kathleen would like a ride out to look at the whales with me?"

"Not the time, Billy. Ye can worry about that later." He paused while the waiter put down the coffee and walked away. "Flaherty said you didn't know about the Mountbatten incident. Is that right?"

Billy nodded, but said nothing as he reached for his cup.

"August 1979 it was and it was a black day for the British. We mounted two spectaculars. One each side of the island. O'Connell had the west side and I was away in the east. His target was Lord Louis Mountbatten. He was a war hero and related to the British royal family so the newspapers and the TV were going to report on him for sure. He had a summer home over the border in the Republic at Classiebawn Castle in County Sligo. He kept a boat in the harbour there and used to spend his summer holidays not twelve miles from the border with the north.

"Anyway, the Army Council decided he was taking liberties by being there, so it was decided to deal with him. O'Connell and a couple of the boys went down to scout out what was what and to make a plan. Tommy McMahon came up with the plan and O'Connell agreed it. They decided they were going to take him when he was on his boat. Thirty feet long and made of wood, it was never going to stand up to a bomb.

"They snuck on board during the night and planted a fifty-pounder right under the steering wheel where they knew Mountbatten would be; him being an ex-Navy man he would always be the one to steer. So anyway, they got the bomb in place and went up onto the headland to watch for it leaving. Tommy had the radio control with him and he was to fire it when O'Connell decided the time was right."

Driscoll sipped his coffee. "So then Mountbatten and his guests got on board and cast off. They were going out lobster potting and tuna fishing, so it's said. O'Connell waited until the boat was close so they could watch the explosion and then he gave Tommy the word. It worked a treat and the boat was blown to bits and scattered across the sea. Mountbatten had his legs just about blown off with the force from underneath him and he ended up in the water. A fishing boat picked him up, but he was dead before they got him to shore. They had an old lady of eighty-three with them and she was killed outright. His grandson was killed and so was a local boy who was earning summer money by working on the boat for Mountbatten."

Billy set his cup down. "How old were the boys?"

"The grandson, Nicholas, was fourteen, and the local boy, Paul Maxwell, was fifteen."

"O'Connell seems to have made a habit of killing children."

"Billy, you need to understand, it's what the Yanks call collateral damage. Anyhow, the press went crazy as we expected and Gerry Adams made a speech about how Mountbatten deserved it. He got a funeral at Westminster Abbey in the September and the press made a big fuss about that again. Tommy got arrested and went to jail for it, but he never said a word about the others who were there that day."

"And what were you doing while this was going on?"

Driscoll smiled. "Ah well, we'd decided to bracket the country so the British wouldn't know where to go next. I was over in the east at Warrenpoint, down on the border with the Republic, just at the head of Carlingford Loch. Four of us there were and we set a bomb by the side of the road where we knew the army came past on their patrols. It was about five hundred

61

pounds of a fertilizer bomb and we had it mounted on a truck and covered in hay bales. The young lass we had with us was down the road as a lookout, to call us when the army were on the way. The other two, Joe and Brendan, went across the border into the south with the radio control and waited. Me, I went into hiding in a hedgerow overlooking the site with a radio and waited.

"We got the call from the girl that there was a small convoy coming along. It was a Land Rover and two trucks. We were ready and as the last truck was alongside the hay wagon the boys triggered the bomb. My God, it was a hell of a noise. There was a huge yellow flash and the army truck was blown on its side across the road with bodies scatted all over the damn place. I lay there with my ears ringing and waited for my part of the plan.

"We had been watching what the army did when one of these bombs went off, so we knew what to expect. Sure enough, more squaddies arrived and set up a command position by the gatehouse on the other side of the road. A rapid reaction force arrived and started to help the wounded, but still I waited. One of their little helicopters flew in and delivered a senior officer, a Lieutenant Colonel I think, and he took over the scene. I could see him issuing orders and talking on the radio. I waited until he was by the gatehouse with a bunch of men and then it was my time. We had laid explosives in milk churns by the gatehouse, about eight hundred pounds I think it was, and I triggered it.

"The gatehouse was blown to bits and pieces of granite flew all over. I was lying inside my bush and there were pieces of bloody meat landing all round me. When I looked up there were body parts hanging off the trees and plastered everywhere. There was one of the bigger helicopters there by then, evacuating wounded. It got hit, but it didn't go down, unfortunately. While everyone on the ground was stunned I got the hell out of there. Joe and Brendan did the same and jumped on their motorbike to get away. The Garda stopped them, but they were let go a bit later for lack of proof."

Billy sat very still and looked at Driscoll. "So how many were killed?"

"Eighteen, and six with what they call life-changing injuries. I found out later that they couldn't find anything of the Lieutenant Colonel; seems he had been vaporised by the blast. They had to put divers into the Newry River to find some of the body parts."

"But you and Joe and Brendan got away with it?"

"Aye. Joe was arrested later for explosive charges to do with something else and he did some time in jail. Poor old Brendan was killed when a bomb he was transporting went off too early. They got my name from an informer and that's when I high-tailed it over here. I didn't want the SAS to come knocking on my door in the middle of the night."

Chapter 15

The Black Rose was already filling rapidly as they arrived. Billy pushed his way through the friendly crowd, careful to keep his old guitar from being damaged. He reached the performance area and found that a stool had already been put out for him and a table right at the front had a reserved notice on it. He looked out over the crowd and saw Kathleen and two of her friends pushing their way through towards him. He waved and pointed down to the table.

She smiled up at him as she sat down and he saw that her friends were whispering and glancing at him. He managed to attract the attention of one of the waiters and got a round of drinks brought to the table for them, before he started to set himself up.

He strummed his guitar a couple of times and the room quieted as the heads turned towards him. He smiled and told his opening joke about the tuning. He heard a small groan from Kathleen as she heard it and he grinned down at her. With the guitar back in tune he launched into 'The Minstrel Boy' as usual. As he sang he knew this was a good crowd. They were already swaying in time to the old tune and some had started to join in with the chorus.

Three songs into his set and the crowd were roaring along to the old songs. He felt he could have walked off the stage and nobody would have noticed. He looked down and Kathleen and her friends were singing along as well. She stopped and smiled broadly at him; he winked and carried on. Just for a change he launched into 'Some Say the Devil is Dead'. The crowd didn't seem to know that one, but they picked up the chorus rapidly and once again they were singing along with him.

He finished his first set and climbed down from the stage to speak to Kathleen. The audience were still applauding as he moved through them and he was patted on the back by a number of appreciative people. He sat with Kathleen and her friends and free drinks arrived from the bar. As the break ended Flaherty climbed onto the stage and ran through his routine of describing British atrocities. Billy looked around the room and saw that the audience were not happy with this. Clearly they were too aware to fall for the guff this time. By the time he got back up to sing the mood in the room had changed and it took him two or three songs to get the people singing again and reacting as they had.

As he finished the last verse of 'The Fields of Athenry' he could see that Flaherty was irritated and ready to leave. He and Driscoll passed through the room with the collecting buckets and Billy could see that both men were flushed and not happy with the response they were getting.

Kathleen's friends left and he sat quietly at the table talking to her. Flaherty came to them in a foul temper and stood looking down at Billy.

"Time we were gone, Billy. I want to be out of this place."

"Sit down, Paddy. I want you to meet Kathleen."

Flaherty glanced at the girl who was smiling at him. "I'm not interested in getting involved in your love life. Now come on, we've got a big day tomorrow."

Billy saw Kathleen's face fall. "Will you stay here a minute, love? I need to speak to Paddy. I'll be right back."

He stood up and nodded towards the door. The two of them walked through the crowd and into the street, with Driscoll trailing after them.

Billy waited until the door of the pub had closed before he spoke. "Just what the hell was that? You had no bloody right at all to speak to me like that in front of a friend."

Flaherty spat into the gutter. "I don't give a flying fuck for your girlfriend and you need to concentrate on the job we are here to do."

Billy was about to punch Flaherty when Driscoll grabbed his arm. "Not a good idea, Billy boy."

The younger man shook himself free and stepped up to Flaherty. "You want publicity for this job you are so keen on? Right then, so how would you like to see me being interviewed on the local TV? That suit you would it? Well, as well as being a friend of mine Kathleen works for the local TV station and is speaking to her boss about it. Unless she takes offence at being treated like shit by you."

Flaherty opened his mouth to speak, but Billy had already spun on his heel and was walking back into the pub.

When Driscoll came back and sat down at the table Billy was holding Kathleen's hand and speaking quietly to her. They both stopped and looked at the older man without speaking.

"Well, that was awkward. Flaherty feels a complete eejit after Billy put him straight. I think he's too embarrassed to come back in here so I sent him home. How would you two like to walk down to the Long Wharf and I'll buy you a drink in the Marriott bar? There's a grand view over the harbour with all the lights on at this time of night."

Kathleen nodded. "That might be nice. I haven't been in there for a long time."

Billy stood and held out his hand to help Kathleen up. He nodded to Driscoll and they walked out of the bar onto State Street. They walked in silence for a while until they reached the doors of the Marriott Hotel.

Driscoll stopped and let them walk on a pace or two. "Look, I feel like the fifth wheel on a wagon here. You two want to talk, so you go on and I'll head back to the house to hold Flaherty's hand. After a couple of wets in the bar, of course." He reached into his pocket and handed a few dollar notes to Billy. "You won your bet, by the way, so there's your winnings."

Billy looked down at the $100 as Driscoll walked away. He nearly called him back, but decided not to. Then he walked into the hotel with Kathleen and up the escalator to the bar with the view over the harbour. Driscoll had been right: it was a fine view and romantic for two young people.

Chapter 16

The clock on the staircase was chiming two when Billy opened the front door and came into the house. He was being quiet, so as not to wake anyone, when he saw the dim light in the living room. He walked in to find Flaherty sitting in the armchair nursing a whiskey in a cut glass tumbler.

"You want a drink, Billy?"

"No, I'm good."

"Yes, you are. You're bloody good and it was me that screwed up the gig tonight. That's what put me in a foul temper and I'm sorry I was rude to your friend. Is she really going to get you on the local TV?"

"I'm not sure. We didn't talk about it after your performance."

"I've said I'm sorry, so give me a bloody break, will you? I'll apologise to her next time I see her. Is she coming to the next show?"

"Yes, she's coming."

"Good. I'll make it right with her then. That's what I wanted to say really, so now I'm for me bed. Did you see Driscoll, by the way? He's not in yet."

"Last time I saw him he was heading back towards the Black Rose. Maybe they're having a lock-in after tonight. I think they made a few bucks."

"Probably. Anyway, I'll see you in the morning and I really am sorry I was a pain in the arse."

Billy watched Flaherty stumble to the stairs and up to his room, then picked up the empty glass and the whiskey bottle. He put the bottle back in the drinks cupboard and took the glass through to the kitchen to wash it. As he was walking back to the stairs to get to his bed he saw the blue and red flashing lights through the frosted glass of the front door. The shadow of a big man flickered on the glass as the bell rang.

He opened it to find himself facing a police patrolman. "Good morning, sir. Do you know a Peter Driscoll?"

Billy nodded and stepped back to let the officer in. "I do. This is his house. We're staying with him for a few days."

"Do you know where he was tonight, sir?"

"Of course. He was with us at the Black Rose pub. I was singing there and he came to watch."

"You said us. Who else is that?"

"Mr Flaherty. I suppose he's what you'd call my manager."

"And where would he be?"

"He'll be in his bed upstairs. He had a bit too much to drink, so he's probably sleeping soundly by now. What's this about anyway?"

"We found Mr Driscoll's body about an hour ago down near the harbour."

"His body? Does that mean he's ..."

The policeman nodded. "He's dead, sir. Shot through the back of the head at close range judging by the burn marks around the wound."

70

"Oh, Dear Lord! Do you know who did it? Was it a robbery?"

"His wallet was still there and had money in it, so no, it wasn't a robbery. It looks like a deliberate hit. Do you know what Mr Driscoll did for a living that might have caused this?"

Billy sat down on the stairs and looked up at the officer. "He was retired. He used to work back home in Ireland, but I don't know what business he was in. I'm sorry."

"I see, and where were you around midnight, sir?"

Billy blinked "Me? You think I might have done it?"

"Just a routine question, sir. So where were you?"

Billy thought for a second. "Around midnight I was in the bar at the Marriott Long Wharf."

"Not far from where we found the body then. Can anybody verify that you were there and for how long?"

"Yes, I was with Miss Kathleen Riley all evening to about half past one this morning. I took her home and then walked back here. Got in about fifteen minutes ago."

The police officer made notes as he stood in the hallway. "And what about Mr Flaherty, is it? Where was he?"

"I couldn't say. He left us at the Black Rose and came back here."

The officer looked up from his notes. "Right then. You'll both have to come down to the station now, so we can conduct a test to see if either of you have fired a gun."

"Now?"

"Now."

Chapter 17

He knew the GSR test on his hands must have been negative, but the police were still not satisfied. He checked his watch again. Almost six o'clock in the morning. He had been there for almost four hours answering the same questions again and again. He wondered how Flaherty was faring. He had been almost incoherent when dragged out of his bed and poured into the back of a police cruiser. Billy hadn't realised until then just how drunk the older man was.

The big black detective came back into the interview room. He sat across the table and handed Billy a coffee. "Long night, huh?"

Billy sipped the coffee and almost spat the disgusting brew back into the cup. "You always drink this swill?"

The detective laughed. "Sorry about that. It's been stewing for a couple of hours. They'll make some fresh when the shift changes."

Billy put the paper cup down and leaned on the table. "Look, officer, I've answered all your questions and I'm damned sure there was no gunshot residue on me when you did the swabs. I've never fired a gun in my life, so there couldn't be."

The detective leaned his chair backwards. "And?"

"And, so why am I still here? I don't know anything about Driscoll's killing. He was a friend of mine, for heaven's sake. He got me the gigs I'm playing around Boston, so why the hell would I want to kill him anyway?"

The detective's chair rocked forward and he looked into Billy's eyes. "Now that's a real good question. We looked into your friend Driscoll. Seems the British have been looking for him for years. They seem to think he has some serious questions to answer, or he had till this morning."

"What kind of questions?"

"Seems they think he's an IRA terrorist and still has some killings to answer for, or that's what we got back from our questions."

Billy snorted. "The Troubles in Ireland have been over for years, man. Driscoll is just an old man living out his retirement in a place where he won't have to live with the problems we still have in Ireland."

The detective sat quietly for a moment and then reached into the top pocket of his jacket. He pulled out a business card and flipped it across the table to Billy. It spun across the scarred surface and came to rest right way up and facing him. He looked down at it and said nothing.

"What do you know about that? What does AVNI mean? Does it stand for something? And what does that hand mean?"

Billy leaned back and sighed. "I watched a lot of American cop shows on the TV. They always say 'don't ask a question unless you know the answer.'"

"So let's hear if I have the right answer then."

"OK. Well, I don't know what AVNI means. The red hand is the symbol of Ulster according to the official flag. It comes from an old Irish legend."

"Ulster?"

"Ulster is the six counties of Ireland that are under British rule. You probably call it Northern Ireland."

"What about the rest of it?"

"The rest? Oh right. The same card was found on the body of my stepdad. He'd been killed and tortured. The police thought it might be a revenge killing by the SAS or somebody like that. Then a couple of weeks ago another person who was helping us with the tour was found with his throat cut in an alley in New York. He had one of those cards as well."

"SAS, that's Special Forces, yes?"

"That's right."

"So why would they kill your stepdad?"

"Probably the same as Driscoll: he was in the IRA many years ago and they never caught him. He was named by a tout, that's what we call an informer, but there was never any solid proof, so he wasn't arrested."

The detective stood up and retrieved the card. "That's what your friend Flaherty said as well. You can go and take him with you. You might want to stop and get him some Tylenol on your way. He's got one hell of a hangover. I'd say don't leave town, but Flaherty says you have gigs lined up all over the place. The chief says you can carry on with the tour as long as you keep me

75

informed of where you are. We may need you for the trial when we catch this son of a bitch."

"You think you're going to catch him?"

"Truthfully? Probably not, unless he does it again. We've not got a lot to go on in the way of clues or information."

Billy went down the dirty hallway and collected Flaherty from the bench by the desk sergeant's station. The detective was right; he was suffering badly from the whiskey and lack of sleep. He took his arm and helped him out of the police station into the cool of the morning. The fresh air revived Flaherty a little and they got a cab to Driscoll's place. While Billy was making the coffee he heard Flaherty on the phone, but couldn't hear what was being said.

Chapter 18

Billy closed the front door and walked towards the stairs. "In here, Billy!"

He turned and walked into the living room. Flaherty was sitting in front of the TV with the inevitable whiskey at his elbow. "Somebody I want you to meet, Billy."

The living room door closed and he realised that there was someone who had been standing behind it. "Bit of a dramatic entrance, don't you think, Paddy?"

"This is O'Shea. The boys have sent him over to have a word with you."

The stranger nodded, but said nothing. Billy looked the man up and down. He was of middling height, middling build and had an unmemorable face. He looked around fifty years old, but there was no trace of beer belly in his taut figure.

"Why would you want to talk with me?"

Flaherty stood up and faced him. "There's three of our volunteers dead and the common factor is you. We want to know what you know about it."

Billy shrugged. "This is the same conversation I had with the Boston PD two nights ago. I don't know what AVNI is and I don't have any idea what's going on."

The violent punch to his kidneys took him by surprise. He was bent backwards by the blow and fell to the floor gasping in pain. As he tried to catch his breath and rise, the kick to his ribs knocked him over again. He looked up to see

O'Shea standing over him with a small smile playing around his lips.

"You see, I don't ask politely like the police, and I don't read you your rights. You're going to tell me what I want to know and that's a fact, boy."

The foot shot forward again and caught the same ribs it had hit before. The pain was intense and Billy groaned as he rolled on the floor. Flaherty walked around to stand next to O'Shea and looked down at Billy.

"The sooner you tell him the truth the sooner this stops, Billy. Now be sensible and talk." He glanced at O'Shea. "Remember, leave his face and his fingers alone; he still has to be able to play, if we let him live."

Billy got his breath back and leaned on one elbow. "I've told you, I know damn all about what's going on. Why don't you find out what the hell AVNI means? Then you've got a sensible place to start."

O'Shea stamped on his ankle and the pain shot up his leg, making him cry out. Before he could do any more his other ankle had been kicked with what felt like a steel-toe-capped boot.

"You mind if he's limping?"

Flaherty walked towards the door. "Just get the truth and don't take all night about it."

Billy turned his head to watch Flaherty leave, and then looked up at O'Shea. "So this is what I get for helping you bastards, is it?"

He was nearly able to move out of the way of the next kick, but he misjudged where it was going and left his right knee exposed. The pain shot through him again and he yelled his pain.

O'Shea leaned against the back of the big TV chair. "This can all be over, you know. Just tell me who else is involved in this. It's so easy."

Billy gripped the knee that was still sending the agony stabbing through him. "I've done nothing, you moron, and there's nobody involved with me. I have no clue what the hell AVNI is. I'm just here to raise money for the boys. I'm working for the cause, for Christ's sake."

O'Shea grinned. "Well, that's for me to find out, ain't it? You can save yourself a world of pain if you just tell me now, boy."

Billy rolled to get away and his attacker dropped on his back, his bony knee pounding into his already bruised kidneys. He screamed and passed out. When he came round he found he was sitting in a dining chair with his feet and hands bound tightly to the wood. O'Shea was watching the TV and smiled as he looked across at him.

"Welcome back. Have a nice little sleep, did we?"

"Where's Flaherty? Get him in here."

"Now why would I do that, boy? We're just getting started."

The door opened and Flaherty stood there with a glass in his hand. "I heard you yell my name. What do you want?"

"Why the bloody hell are you doing this? What makes you think I've got anything to do with the killings? Come on, before your sadistic pal here screws everything up."

"Screws what up?"

"I'm raising money for the cause because you asked me to. I've seen how much is going in the collecting buckets and this is my bloody reward?"

Flaherty sat down and sighed. "Billy, you are the only thing common to all three killings."

"Go on then, lay it out for me. O'Shea, you need to listen to this as well."

"All right then. The first of the AVNI killings was Seamus, your da. So there's the first connection. O'Connell was next and you were in his apartment. Then Driscoll here in Boston. He'd been walking with you and that Kathleen before he turned up dead."

"Did you hear all that, O'Shea?"

"I did, so what? Are you going to confess now?"

"In the face of such overwhelming evidence, how can I not? Seamus Murphy was a big man, wasn't he? Strong, tough and ruthless. He was your friend, wasn't he? Well, when he died I was twelve feckin years old. How do you imagine I overpowered him? O'Connell now, another of your friends from way back, right? I was in the apartment when he was killed. When the police came knocking I never let on about you, did I? And then Driscoll. You were having some kind of temper tantrum and he grabbed your arm and had a word before you stormed out of the pub. I was with Kathleen until way after Driscoll had been found, so I have an alibi. You getting all this, O'Shea?"

Flaherty sighed. "What's your point, Billy?"

"I was too young to have done me da, but you weren't. O'Connell was your old friend, not mine. I had no reason to kill him. Shit, I hardly knew the man, but you did from way back. Then there's Driscoll. I have an alibi that was good enough for the Boston PD, so where's your alibi, Flaherty? You had words with him earlier in the evening and stormed out. Who can prove where you were after that?"

"And why in the name of all that's holy would I want to kill them?"

Billy smiled at O'Shea. "You got it yet, man? All three of them knew Flaherty from the old days. How about all three of them knew things that could get him jailed for a bloody long time? Maybe the Unionists would like to know some of the things he did to their people? That would spare you any jail time, wouldn't it, Flaherty?"

"And what about AVNI? What's that supposed to mean to me?"

"As Mr O'Shea has heard me say, I have no idea what AVNI is. Maybe you do?"

"Bloody stupid!"

"Is it now? Why don't we ask Mr O'Shea here? How about you spend a couple of hours kicking the shit out of Flaherty and find out what he knows?"

O'Shea raised an eyebrow at Flaherty. "The boy makes some interesting points there, Paddy. Do ye think maybe ye've been a little hasty?"

"It's not hasty at all. This bastard is just pissed off at me because he made a fool of himself in the Black Rose and now I've been punished for it."

"That's not true, Billy. I apologised for that."

O'Shea uncurled himself from the chair he had been sitting in to listen. "Either way, I'll be having a word with the boys and see what they say about all this."

"Am I supposed to stay tied to this bloody chair then?"

O'Shea smiled his evil smile. "There's a knife on the table, Flaherty. You can use it on the ropes instead of what I had planned."

As the torturer walked out of the room Flaherty picked up the knife and sliced through the bonds that held Billy. He stepped back as Billy struggled to stand on his injured legs and massaged his wrists.

"Billy, I ..."

"Don't speak to me, you bastard. That piece of shit was just doing the job the boys gave him, but you called him in on me. Don't you ever dream that I'll forget that."

Chapter 19

Sleep had been difficult with the pain in his back and legs. Turning over in the bed had him biting his lip to keep from screaming. The morning shone through the window and found him awake again and feeling like hell, but his bladder forced him to get up. Just moving was a struggle and he limped to the bathroom. As he urinated, he had to grip the shelf beside him to keep from moaning with the agony.

He blundered back to the bedroom and collapsed on the small chair in the corner. He stayed still to let the pain ease, and then took his clothes from the hook beside him and slowly dressed. The heavy shoes were too much for his damaged feet, so he made his way, painfully slowly, down the stairs in his bare feet. Supporting himself on the passage wall, he made it from the bottom of the stairs to the kitchen. O'Shea and Flaherty were already sitting at the breakfast table when he opened the door.

O'Shea smiled at him as he entered. "Now then, Billy, how's yerself this fine morning?"

"How do you bloody imagine I am after the kicking?"

"You shouldn't take it personally, Bill. We just have to know we can trust you."

"You call this trust?"

O'Shea put down his coffee mug. "I've made a judgement and I've vouched for you to the boys back home. You'll not be getting any more trouble."

Billy nodded towards Flaherty. "And what about that piece of dog shit?"

"Ah, see now, they trust him from way back. He's been part of the command structure for a long time. Although they do think he may have been a little previous calling me in to speak to you."

Flaherty finally managed to look at Billy. "Will you be wanting a coffee? I'll get it for you."

"Don't bother. I want bugger all from you. I'll get it for meself."

He poured the coffee from the jug on the machine and leaned against the kitchen counter to sip it. The dark liquid warmed him as it slid down his throat and he looked out of the window to see it was a bright day with just a few clouds.

"You looking forward to the gig tonight, Billy?" Flaherty asked.

Billy turned his head towards the older man very slowly. "Are you out of your tiny bloody mind? I'm struggling to walk and it hurts like hell when I piss. But you think I'm going to hop up on stage and sing jolly feckin rebel songs for your benefit?"

Flaherty paused, unsure of himself in the face of such venom. "We've got a booking and people are expecting us."

"You can go and take a running jump at yerself. I'm going no place until I can walk properly and piss without crying."

Flaherty looked to O'Shea for support, but found none. "Did you really expect him to be happy about last night, Paddy?"

"How long will you be before you can sing then, Billy? I'll need to change our bookings and we've got to think about what we are going to do about Seattle."

Billy pushed himself away from the counter and started to hobble to the door. "Ask the bloody expert. He's got more experience of this than me."

Flaherty sat and looked at the closing door, then glanced at O'Shea. "Well? What do you think?"

"He'll be feeling better in a week or so is my guess."

"A bloody week?"

"Hey, you said you wanted him worked over to find the truth, and now you've got it you don't like it. That's not my problem. You were the one who was hasty, not me."

Chapter 20

O'Shea had been almost right and after eight days Billy felt ready to get up on stage and sing again. He had told Kathleen he had been mugged, but refused to involve the police when she suggested it. Flaherty had stayed out of the way as much as possible to allow him time to cool down, but he was in no mood to forgive and forget. O'Shea had been instructed to stay on as some form of bodyguard.

"So then, since we seem to be working together now, what do you do when you're not trying to beat information out of people?"

O'Shea looked up from the newspaper. "I make problems go away. I keep the volunteers and others from breaking the rules."

"Is that needed anymore? I could see the point during the Troubles, but now it's all over?"

"I thought you were from Belfast?"

"I am."

"Then you know it's not over. It's never over until Ireland is a united, socialist republic. Right now the boys are doing other tasks. The drugs and the protection, to keep the funds building up for when we are ready. You surely didn't think you were the only one helping to build the war chest, now did you?"

Billy shrugged. "I hadn't really thought about it. I was just enjoying the singing and seeing new places."

"You keep on doing that, you make a fine cover for the next part."

"What next part?"

O'Shea grinned. "You'll see, but for now just sing the songs and keep the collection buckets filling. I'm interested to see a performance tonight. A couple more here in Boston and then we're away to Seattle. I'm told it's a nice town."

The show went well and the collection buckets were filled nicely when Flaherty and O'Shea walked them around the crowd. Kathleen was working, so she wasn't in the audience, which made it less fun. Billy made up for it by singing 'McAlpine's Fusiliers' and watching O'Shea's face at the back of the crowd as he reached the verse that went:-

"I remember the day that the fair O'Shea fell into a concrete stairs,

What the horse face said when he saw him dead,

Well, it wasn't what the rich called prayers.

'I'm a navvy short' was the one retort that reached unto my ears."

The IRA enforcer smiled widely and nodded at Billy before toasting him with the beer he had in his hand. It seemed the thug had a sense of humour after all.

The show ended and Billy sat at the table while the other two collected the final donations and brought it back to be counted. He drank his first beer of the night and eased his dry throat.

O'Shea looked up as he finished counting. "That's a strange expression you have on your face there, Billy. What's that about?"

"Something you said earlier on today. You said you kept volunteers and others from breaking the rules. What did you mean by others?"

"Anyone who did things the boys didn't like. We needed the community to stay on side, if you like, so they had to toe the line, or be made to."

"Like what?"

Chapter 21
7 December 1972

"There was a widow living in the Divis Flats in Belfast, Jean McConville. She had ten kids, but the boys had decided we had to make an example of her to keep the rest in line."

"Why her?"

O'Shea took a sip of his beer. "Well see now, I was never too certain what the reason was. The boys put the word out that she was an informer for the army and was passing information to them. Then others said it was because she had comforted a badly injured soldier in the street one day. I was never sure which was true."

"So you didn't ask?"

"Not my job to ask, son. I was told to go down to the border with the Republic and do the job there. They sent four women volunteers to her flat and dragged her out. They put her in the car and drove down to the border and then to Shellinghill Beach. They'd questioned her on the way south so she was a bit knocked about when they got her out of the car."

"Then what?"

"She was swearing that she had never informed on anybody. Then she told me her son Robbie was in the Official IRA and was in the Long Kesh internment camp, so she'd never betray him or his friends. Turns out that was true, he was locked up in the Kesh. Anyway, it didn't matter what she told me, I'd been given my orders. Two of the boys from south of the border had been along and dug a grave just above the beach. The women walked her over to it and I shot her. She fell in and we pushed the sand back on top of her so that was that for that night. The Army Council decided not to leave her body in the street the way we usually did to encourage the rest. Because she was the mother of ten children they had her buried and then denied they knew anything about it. But we made sure the people in Divis Flats knew the score."

"What about the kids?"

"Ah, now that was a bit sad. Some of them were taken into care and there was some abuse in the social services home."

Billy sat quietly for a moment or two. "You said that was that for that night. What did you mean?"

"The family lobbied the government for years and eventually they issued a statement that she had never been an informant. The kids also kept asking us to tell them where the body was. It was uncovered by a storm in 2003. After the Good Friday Agreement the IRA admitted that we had done it and we claimed that she was an informant. They put out a tale that they had searched her flat and found a transmitter. All bollocks, of course, but it was all over by then."

"How could you do it? You left ten kids alone in the world. No ma, no da, nothing."

"It was how things were back then."

"And now?"

"Nothing changes, boy. We need to maintain control. We need the people to do as they're told. They know what happens if they don't."

Chapter 22

"O'Shea was telling me about a killing he did."

Flaherty chortled. "Just the one? If that one put notches on his gun he'd need a new gun and probably more than one."

"How's that?"

"O'Shea started killing early on in the Troubles and he was good at it. That's why they made him the enforcer. No bombs or mortars for that one. He shot them or cut them. Up close and personal whenever he could."

Billy sat down heavily. "And that's the one you've got coming round with us?"

Flaherty shook his head. "Not my choice. The boys back home have decided we need a minder. They don't want any more of the old boys getting hit and they don't trust you and me as much as they did. That's the problem when people get killed around you, it breeds distrust, so it does."

"And if he thinks we're stepping out of line?"

"Don't go there, Billy. You really don't want to know the answer."

Billy looked down at his hand and then back to Flaherty. "So where is he anyway? Shouldn't we be packing ready for tomorrow?"

"He said he wanted to have a drink or two away from this house. He'll be back in time for the flight to Seattle. It's not as if he has much stuff to pack now, is it?"

"Right then, I'm for me bed and a good night's sleep. Do we have someone to set us up in Seattle?"

Flaherty nodded and put his glass down on the side table by his chair. "We have people everywhere. A lot of people left Ireland during the Troubles, but we keep in touch and they know they owe us."

Billy stood and walked to the door. "I'll see you in the morning. So you know, I'll be going to see Kathleen before the flight, but I won't be long."

"Not a problem, Billy. Remember to remind her about getting you that spot on her TV show. We'll swing back into Boston for it. Say goodbye from me, eh? And I'll take your bags to the airport if you want to meet me there?"

Billy nodded and went up to his bed. He struggled to sleep as he thought about what O'Shea and the others had told him about the Troubles. Even living in Belfast he hadn't heard all the stories and they worried him.

It was Flaherty's turn to make the coffee for breakfast and Billy had to admit he made a good job of it. He sat at the small round table in the kitchen eating his pancakes and sipping at the dark brew.

"What time did O'Shea get back in last night?"

Flaherty put down his coffee mug and reached for the maple syrup. "He's not back yet. Seems like he's really tying one on. He'll be like a bear with a sore head when he does get here.

Might be an idea to stay out of his way. He's got a fine temper on him when he's had a few too many."

Billy stood up and took his plate to the sink. "Mind if I leave you with the dishes? I'm spending all the morning and then some with Kathleen. I'll see you out at Logan airport."

"Don't forget the flight is at 18:05 with Alaska Airlines. You need to be there two hours before."

"What about the other end?"

"We land at 21:29 according to the booking. We'll stay one night in the Embassy Suites in Tacoma and our contact will be there to pick us up in the morning. You have a good day, eh?"

The day with Kathleen taking him around the sights of Boston passed all too quickly and she dropped him off at the airport well in time for the flight. The kiss took too long and a police officer tapped on the roof to get the car moving. He watched her drive away and then walked into the terminal building. Flaherty was waiting for him, but there was no sign of O'Shea.

"So where is he then?"

"No idea. I rang his cell phone, but it went straight to voicemail every time. He hadn't packed, so I left his bags for him to deal with."

"So what do we do then?"

Flaherty shrugged. "We check in and go and catch the plane. He should be along anytime now, but we can't afford to miss the flight just because he's too drunk to get here."

Billy lifted his bags from the floor. "You think that's what it is?"

"Probably, but either way we need to go now."

They checked in and went through the usual rigmarole of getting through the security barriers. Once through, Billy put his shoes on and looked back over the security area for O'Shea.

"You'd think they'd have to buy you dinner before putting their hands in those places, wouldn't you? I think I'd like to watch O'Shea go through that performance."

Flaherty smiled. "Maybe not a good idea. He'll be steaming angry if they do the same to him and I don't want to catch the blame."

The departure boards rolled up and their aircraft showed as boarding about forty minutes later. They walked down to the gate and waited to be checked through. Both of them kept looking back down the airport concourse to see O'Shea.

As they reached the final check-in desk Flaherty shrugged. "He'll just have to find another flight. Means we get three seats between us so that should be better."

Even as the crew started the safety demonstration, Billy expected to see O'Shea blunder through the cabin door and on to the aircraft. He gave up as he saw the airport rolling slowly past the window as they were pushed back from the stand. Flaherty was asleep almost before they took off and Billy watched the in-flight movies until the seat belt signs came on and they made their approach to SeaTac airport outside Seattle.

The white courtesy bus took them to the hotel and they checked in. Billy was amazed by the huge atrium surrounded by balconies. The glass lift took them up and he walked around to his room at the back of the hotel. As he walked inside he was surprised to find there was no bed. He was in a sitting room. He walked on and found a small kitchen and a bathroom before he walked into the bedroom with the two king-size beds. He looked out of the window across the countryside behind the hotel and then the tiredness took him and he lay down for the night.

The mournful train horn woke him in the early hours and he went to the window to see a freight train passing by. He turned on the TV and found a news channel. A murder in Boston would not normally have made it onto a news broadcast in Seattle, but the body had been found in the Charleston Navy Yard bumping up against the wooden hull of the USS *Constitution*. Billy sat on the end of the bed and watched as the bulletin repeated on different channels. There was no mention of a name for the victim, but the sinking feeling in his stomach told him that this was too much of a coincidence.

Chapter 23

He got dressed and walked around the balcony to the glass elevator. As he rode it down he saw Flaherty across the atrium floor, standing by the counter where the chef was making omelettes to order. By the time he got there his companion had got his breakfast and was heading for a table beside an artificial pond. Billy poured himself a coffee and walked across to join him.

As he pulled the chair out Flaherty looked up from his breakfast. "You'll need more than a coffee, Billy. You should try one of these. The cook makes them any way you want. Really good, but the bacon is lethal. Every time I try and cut it the bloody stuff shatters. I've got fragments halfway across the room."

"I'll get breakfast in a minute. I think we've got a problem."

Flaherty spoke around the mouthful of egg. "What's that then?"

"There's been a murder in Boston. It's on the TV news. They found the body in the harbour next to that wooden ship they have there."

"Why would that concern us?"

"Take a look round, man. Can you see O'Shea? These killings are following us like a bad smell."

Flaherty chuckled and shook his head. "You don't know O'Shea. He's a stone-cold killer. Nobody knows how many he took out during the Troubles. I doubt if even he knows. It would have to be someone pretty special to take him."

Billy picked up his coffee. "I thought you said the SAS were after revenge? Are they special enough for you? Maybe they're the ones calling themselves AVNI?"

Flaherty slowed and put down his fork before leaning back in his chair. "Yeah, they'd be special enough, and Lord knows they would want him, if they knew the things he'd done. I only know some of them, but they'd be the ones to piss off the army and the UVF."

"See what I mean? When is it our turn? Everywhere we go they are killing people who've been with us. Do we get it next?"

Flaherty pushed the plate away, his appetite gone. "Worse than that, Billy; if the boys back home think we are involved we could be in deep shit. They tend to act first and think about it later. We need to make sure they don't think we're doing this as well as watching our own backs in case AVNI want us too."

"Do we even have a clue what AVNI means? That might tell us something."

Flaherty shook his head. "I've got no idea. Maybe if I ask the intelligence boys if they know? That might make them think twice about blaming us anyway."

Billy watched and couldn't help but smile a little as Flaherty jumped up and scuttled away to where the computers for public use were. He finished his coffee and walked across to where the chef made him an omelette while he topped up the coffee mug. He had finished eating by the time his companion returned.

"I've sent an email to the boys telling them that we suspect the body in Boston might be O'Shea and I've sent another to a friend in Boston. His son is in the police there, so I've asked him to find out what he can."

Billy sipped the last of his coffee. "Of course it might turn out not to be O'Shea. As you say, he's a dangerous guy and it would take someone special to take him out. He'll probably turn up here anytime now with that grin on his face."

"Sure and I hope that's true. But if the British are after us then O'Shea would be the one they wanted all right. Some of the stuff he did wound them up a lot and maybe they haven't forgotten."

Flaherty glanced around to make sure they could not be overheard. "He was the one that did the Islania killing in Germany and he did the one in the garage. I think his best one was the Kingsmill Massacre. I was part of that one as well. Now that was a bloody night, so it was."

"I'll get us another couple of coffees and you can tell me the Kingsmill tale. It's a better one if you were actually there."

Chapter 24
5th January 1976

Flaherty leaned back in his chair and sipped the coffee that Billy handed him. "It's a long time since I've spoken about that night. Must have been '76, I think. Anyway it was the January, I do remember that. Not long after New Year and damned cold. There'd been some killing of Catholics by Loyalists and we wanted to take revenge. Trouble was, there was a ceasefire in place and the IRA leadership had sent the word down that we were to sit on our hands. We couldn't do that, though."

"We set up a checkpoint on the road out of Whitecross in South Armagh. We made it look like an army checkpoint and we even got hold of one of the lads who sounded English. There was a minibus that used to take the workers from the textile mill home after work and that's what we decided to target. We knew there were usually sixteen men in the bus and we knew that four of them who were Catholics got out in Whitecross. The rest were going along to Besbrook.

"Anyway, the bus came over the rise and the lads we had in uniform stopped them in the road. The one who sounded English told them all to get out and line up by the side of the bus so they could be checked. The eleven of us came out of the bushes then and they realised we weren't the army. Then our man asked, 'Who is Catholic?' The daft bastards thought we were Loyalist paramilitaries and tried to stop the one Catholic showing himself.

We found out the one who was a Catholic and gave him the order: 'Get down the road and don't look back!' He ran as if the hounds of hell were after him. I guess he thought we were going to shoot him in the back.

"Once he was clear O'Shea said 'Right!' and we opened fire on the eleven Protestants who were standing there. We had M16s and AR15 rifles and we were right up to them so we couldn't miss and we pumped them full of lead. When they were all down a couple of them were still alive and O'Shea says, 'Finish them off!', so we blasted them again. Automatic fire at that range there was no way any of them could survive, but wouldn't you know it, one of them did. There was one fellah who had eighteen bullets in him and it turns out he was still alive, but he never moved. The clever bastard fooled us.

"So we left the scene with eleven bodies lying in the road with blood washing down the slope in the rain. We found out later that a married couple had driven up and found them. They were praying over the bodies when they heard a noise and found the one who was alive had crawled into a ditch. He got picked up in an ambulance and taken to Newry. Nobody gave a damn for his chances, but against the odds he made it.

"The newspapers said that two of the bodies were so chewed up they wouldn't let the relatives identify them."

"So despite these guys trying to protect their Catholic workmate you still killed them? How the hell can you justify that?"

Flaherty shrugged. "The decision had been made and we needed to send a message. You can't start second-guessing once the operation has started."

"What happened to the ceasefire?"

Flaherty chuckled. "It went on for a while, but it was never going to last long. We phoned in and claimed that we were the 'South Armagh Republican Action Force'. We told them very clearly that we weren't IRA and the IRA command denied it as well. It was quite a while before they found the guns that had been used that night and they were in the hands of IRA men, so our little story got blown away, but by then it was too late to matter."

"I can see why the British would want you and O'Shea for that one."

"Oh, they were pissed off all right. After that they put the SAS into South Armagh for the first time and stepped up operations. Even if the British aren't behind this AVNI thing, then there's still Loyalists who would love to know who did the Kingsmill job."

"Did anybody get arrested for it?

"Nary a one. We all walked away free and clear."

"Until now, maybe. If this AVNI group knows O'Shea did it then maybe they know you did it too."

"Could be. I think I'll go and see if there's a reply to my email."

Chapter 25

Billy watched Flaherty walk across the atrium floor to the computer. He was back about ten minutes later and sat down heavily.

"It looks like it's O'Shea. The police contact says that there was one of those damned AVNI cards in his pocket. He's been smashed over the head from behind with something heavy and blunt and then given a double kneecapping. They think he was conscious when they did that. He was finished off with two to the skull. One went through each eye. Somebody really wanted to send a message with this one."

"It sounds like one of the punishment shootings O'Shea was talking about the other night. Do you think it could be some enemy within the old IRA taking revenge for something? Or maybe it was one of the splinter groups?"

Flaherty leaned back and looked at Billy for a long moment. "I hadn't thought of that. It's possible. Sometimes mistakes were made and we hit the wrong people. People we thought were informing got kneecapped or executed and then we found out later we were wrong about them. That might explain O'Shea, but what about the other two? They were volunteers, but not enforcers."

Billy nodded slowly. "That's true, but this still sounds like the IRA's style. Just like the killing of my da was in their style."

"If it's the British they may be doing it on purpose to divide us. They could be copying our methods to make people think like you about it."

"We still don't know what the AVNI cards are about, though, do we?"

The older man nodded and glanced around him again. "I had a message from the boys as well. They've been digging and they think they know what it might mean. The crossed SLR rifles and the red hand of Ulster make them think it's some British revenge group. They are guessing, but they think AVNI might be 'Army Veterans Northern Ireland' or something similar."

"So the people we worked with and maybe us as well are being targeted by soldiers who served in the province during the Troubles? Why would they start now, after all these years?"

Flaherty sighed and shook his head. "They think it might be as a result of our build-up strategy. I told you we were damaging army morale by going after veterans and trying to prosecute them for shootings that happened forty or fifty years ago? Well, that was working and there's been a drop in people trying to join the army, all good, so it is. But then the older guys who served in Ulster got angry and there's been big demonstrations in support of the guys getting prosecuted. The press has been muzzled and there have been no reports worth a damn in the papers or on TV, and that has made them angrier still."

"So now they've taken to killing people?"

"That's what the command council thinks might be happening."

Billy leaned forward and rested his elbows on the table. "Where does that leave us and why the hell are they coming after people we have worked with?"

"Again they're guessing, but they think these AVNI people have seen that we are fundraising over here and are raising the profile of the struggle again. They think the killings might be a warning and may be a big hint for us to back off."

Billy slumped in his chair and looked across the table. "What are we supposed to do then?"

"We carry on. We don't meet up with our contact here at all. He has arranged gigs for us and will pass the info by email, but we won't see him unless something goes wrong. That way he can't be targeted by these bastards."

"Good thinking – with just one tiny drawback."

"What's that then?"

"That leaves you and me hanging in the breeze if these AVNI people want to have a go and can't find anyone else to have a go at."

"We have to risk it. On the upside we've been told to stay in hotels, so we aren't going to be in anybody's home this time."

Billy smiled. "That's going to eat into the funds we collect, though, eh?"

"I told you the gigs and the collecting buckets were only part of this. Well, tomorrow we are going to see one of the big backers we've got lined up. This guy is a serious player and this is where the real money will be coming from. You're coming along as part of the cover; we are going to tell anyone who asks he's considering booking you for his daughter's birthday party."

Chapter 26

Billy sat in the chair idly flipping through the TV channels while he waited for Flaherty to get in touch with their local contact. The phone rang and he heaved himself up and walked across the room to pick it up.

"Yep?"

"Mister Murphy? This is reception. There's a lady here who says you know her. May we send her up?"

Billy paused in surprise. "I don't know anyone in this town. What's her name?"

The line went silent as the receptionist covered the mouthpiece. "She says she's called Kathleen and you met her in Boston apparently."

"Send her round to the bar, will you? I'll be down in a second."

He grabbed his wallet and pulled the door open. As he walked rapidly along the balcony he looked down into the atrium and saw Kathleen walking past the gift shop in the corner, pulling a small suitcase. He came to a stop and watched her in some amazement. It really was her and he couldn't help but smile. He strode onwards to the glass elevator and rode it down to the ground floor. As the doors slid open he turned to the right and she smiled broadly as she saw him appear.

"Kathleen! How are you here?"

"They call it an airplane, Billy." She smiled.

He grinned at the silly joke. "You know what I mean."

"The station sent me to set you up with our local affiliate. We've run the idea around the local stations we are linked up with and, if it works out, we'll have you on TV coast to coast in time for St Paddy's Day."

Billy could hardly believe what he was hearing. This could be his big break. If he was seen by so many people this could be when the record company saw him.

"Come sit down in the bar and I'll buy you a drink. D'you want something to eat with that?"

"I'll take a chicken sandwich and a beer."

"Sounds good. I'll have the same. You go find a table and I'll see the barman."

He walked across the room with the two beers and sat down. "They'll bring the food over soon, so he says. So tell me about this plan of yours."

She put the beer down and smiled at him. "The way it works is that the smaller local stations share content and if someone has a good idea we all show it, no matter who does the actual recording. You know we wanted to interview you in Boston, but one of the Seattle stations agreed to do it here. My boss sent me over to be the liaison and to make sure we get the credit for finding you."

"So what do we do then?"

"Here come the sandwiches. That was quick. OK, so what happens is that I go into the station and we work out the format we're going to use. I'll brief you and we'll work out when we are going to do it. You'll be fine, it's not as if there's many people there. It'll probably be a small studio, very cosy and friendly."

Billy chewed and swallowed. "Sounds fine to me. What sort of time will Flaherty get for his stories?"

"We're not really interested in Flaherty or his stories. We'll be wanting you to sing a couple of songs and then you'll probably get a few questions about the reasons for the tour. Things like where the money that you collect goes to and who it benefits. Usual stuff."

"So do I get to hear the questions beforehand? Just so I can make sure I know what I'm going to say. I don't want to look an eejit now, do I?"

"They don't usually do that, but I'll see what I can find out for you. I should be able to get the questions for you. I don't want you to perform poorly either."

"That all sounds good. Are you staying here?"

"That was my plan. I guess you'll have plenty of room?"

Billy almost choked on his beer. "You mean you'll stay with me? Oh, that'll be just fine. The luck of the Irish, eh?"

Chapter 27

"You've agreed to what?" Flaherty yelled.

All round the bar, heads turned in their direction. Billy was glad of the table between them or he thought he might have been receiving a fist from Flaherty. The older man's eyes seem to bulge and his face was flushed with anger.

He lowered his voice and almost hissed. "You have no idea what you are doing, ya mutton. They'll try and get you to say something stupid just because it makes better television. If you embarrass us on a coast to coast network, even if it is the smaller stations, the boys back home will be furious. Do ye understand what that means?"

Billy, was a little stunned and sat silent.

"Is there any way of changing this and having me answer the questions, so you just sing?"

"I don't think so. Kathleen said they aren't interested in you, they just want me. That's the way they've sold it to the associated TV stations and that's the way it's been set up here to be filmed."

"When will she be back? I'll see if I can persuade her to get it changed. The last thing she'll want is to get her boyfriend in trouble back home."

Billy shook his head. "Paddy, she doesn't know a damned thing about the realities of Ireland. She's another American with dreams of a misted island homeland. She's too young to understand the Troubles and she certainly doesn't know the IRA is still active. If you tell her the truth it could hurt us badly."

Flaherty was returning to his normal colour as he calmed down and leaned back in his chair. He took a swallow of the ice-cold beer in front of him.

"You might be right. The TV show is an opportunity if it goes right. It could get us the sort of invitations we need apart from the singing gigs."

Billy felt the relief flow through him as Flaherty settled down. "So when are we going to see this big backer you mentioned? Do you still want me to tag along?"

Flaherty nodded and ran his finger through the condensation on his glass. "A car is coming to pick us up this afternoon and take us to meet him. I still want you there as the cover story, in case anybody starts paying too much attention to us. Bring your guitar in case he wants to hear a sample. His daughter may be there as well, so be charming. She seems to be important to him from what I've heard."

"What about Kathleen? Do you want me to try and change the format of the TV interview?"

"Try and get me included. I can tell them the story of the struggle and how we are now pursuing political solutions. They don't need to know the truth. Maybe you shouldn't push it, though. If she stays with what they have planned then I'll sit down with you and get your story straight and you'd better make sure you tell it properly, boy, or we could both end up in the shit."

"Sure, I'll be careful. I can always play dumb and tell them I don't know things."

111

Flaherty nodded slowly. "Keep that one in your back pocket. We don't want them to think we're just thick paddies. Right now, the car should be here in about twenty minutes you go get your guitar and I'll see you in the lobby at half past."

Billy watched Flaherty gulp his beer and leave the room, heading for the elevator. He finished more slowly and walked across to the bar to pay. The barman walked along towards him, wiping a glass as he came.

"Are you OK, sir? That guy you were with seemed a bit loud all of a sudden. I was going to call security for a minute there."

"No problem. We just had a bit of a disagreement, but he's fine now. Keep the change."

Chapter 28

The car pulled into the parking slot in front of the yacht club. Billy climbed out and looked at the mass of expensive-looking boats all stored under cover at their moorings. The chauffeur led them inside to where their host was waiting. He was a large florid-faced man wearing a well-cut two-piece blue suit. He rose from his chair as they came in and walked towards them with his hand out.

"Wonderful to meet you two. Come and sit down, I've got my favourite window table for us."

The view across Puget Sound was spectacular, with the snow-capped mountains just visible on the other side of the water. All across the wide inlet boats were carving white wakes in the blue.

"Very pretty place you have here, Mr ...?"

"You must be Billy? No need for names just yet. Let's see if we are all singing from the same hymn sheet first, eh?"

Billy sat back and kept his peace, while Flaherty leaned forward. "Are we sure this is a secure place to speak?"

"It is. I do a lot of my business here and I vary which table I sit at to make sure nobody has installed electronic ears to check on me. The staff will leave us well alone once we have placed our order. They know the routine."

Flaherty smiled. "All good then. Now Billy here is the reason we are over in the States, if anybody asks. He is singing around the Irish pubs and we are collecting for the Northern Irish Relief Fund. We don't want anybody realising we have bigger ambitions and connecting us with you on that level."

"Here comes the waiter with the menus. Shall I order the wine? They have some rather fine Californian wines to choose from that I favour. I should do, I own shares in some of the best vineyards. The fish is always good here, as is the steak, of course."

Billy ran his eye down the menu. He couldn't believe the prices. His ma could feed the family for a week on what they were charging for one steak. He looked across the table and saw their host was smiling at him.

"Order what you like, son. The company is paying. This meeting is about an investment for our long-term corporate future after all."

The wine came and the large American tasted it and nodded. Billy watched as his glass was filled and then Flaherty's. They placed their order and he asked for the steak. He couldn't wait to see what was so special about meat that cost this much.

Flaherty lifted his glass. "Would you mind if I was to make the toast? To our mutual future prosperity."

The three of them drank and set the glasses down. "Now then, before the waiters come back, let us be clear about what your organisation is offering us. You could also tell me what sort of investment you are looking for to make it all happen."

Flaherty glanced around as he usually did. "Right then, you know the armed struggle stopped back in 1998? Well, more or less stopped. We have kept our capability and we've also made sure our authority on the streets is still in place. More importantly, from your point of view, we've been making sure our people have worked themselves into key positions in the devolved government and in the Republic. Those two things put us in a position to act when the time is right."

"And when will the time be right?"

"Not too long to wait. The British have reduced the size of their army way too much to deal with us effectively when the armed struggle starts up again. On top of that, we have been hounding their soldiers through the courts over incidents during the Troubles. The present troops will have seen that, so they won't be as keen as the old ones were, back in the day. They'll hesitate. On top of that, MI5 are overstretched watching the Muslims in all the big cities on the mainland. We've been giving them encouragement to make trouble and we've also been teaching them to make bombs and to shoot weapons. Part of the money we raise will equip the Muslims, so that they stir things up and make trouble when we are ready. The army in the Republic is small and ineffective, so they are not a problem, but we have infiltrated them as well to be sure."

"So why do you need me and my money?"

"Last time the armed struggle built up over time. The army had time to learn how to deal with it. This time we want to be fully armed and trained so we flood the streets in one great wave. The British will be overwhelmed. The police are hamstrung by having our people in command positions and the army is not ready. We force the referendum north and south of the border and we know we can browbeat the people into voting our way. That gives us legitimacy on the world stage. The British government will be glad to get rid of Ireland when we make it too hot for them to handle."

The American held up his hand for quiet as the waiters approached carrying the lunch. The steak that landed in front of Billy touched each side of the plate and smelled delicious. He looked across at the fish Flaherty had ordered and wondered if he had chosen right. He cut into the meat and took a bite. The juices flowed into his mouth and he knew he had chosen wisely.

"Now then, that all sounds very fine, but what does it get me and my company?"

Flaherty put his fork down reluctantly. "Well now, we are going to form a socialist government. The state will be in control of industry across the island. We will still be in the European Union, so any plants built on our soil will have free access to that market. Businesses owned by Unionists will be nationalised if they are not friendly towards us, and then they can be sold to overseas interests, such as yourself, at knock-down prices. The rate of tax for businesses will be very attractive and the planning laws for building will be in our hands."

"Won't the European Union object to you making such concessions to foreign companies?"

Flaherty shook his head. "Not really. They are so scared of the Troubles starting up again and spilling over into their countries they will back off. Anyway, most of them have got their snouts too deep in the trough to even notice."

"So, to be clear, once you take over we have a free hand during the confusion and chaos of setting up the new Ireland. Once the chaos calms down again we will have our feet firmly under the table."

Flaherty picked up his fork and grinned. "That's about the size of it. You help us and then we help you. Together we can make Ireland prosperous and free. Well, as free as we want it to be."

The American picked up the bottle and leaned across the table. "More wine there, Billy? You shouldn't let your glass get empty when we have so much to celebrate."

He filled all the glasses and picked up his own. He looked at Flaherty over the rim of the crystal wine glass.

"So what's this going to cost me up front? Then again, I assume there will be some considerations for your senior people going forward as well?"

Flaherty chewed the piece of fish in his mouth then swallowed. "Look at it this way, it's an investment. The more you put in now the more grateful we will be when we take over and the more we will feel obliged to help you."

"And what help do you bring to the table?"

117

"What businesses would you like us to take over and sell to you? You could make a list and we could earmark them for you."

"What would you say if I wanted the Harland and Wolff shipyard?"

"Where they built the Titanic and her sister ships? I can't see that being a problem at all, so I can't."

Chapter 29

"Now listen, Billy. I'm going to say it again. Do not mention anything about our commercial fundraising or our plans for after we take over the government of Ireland. You are just here to raise money to look after people who are in need, because of the British victimising us Catholics. You got that?"

Billy sighed. "You told me that again and again. I've got it, all right? I'm not going to say anything dumb about why we are really here."

Flaherty slumped back in the driver's seat and then pointed through the windscreen. "That's the studio and by the look of it Kathleen is waiting outside for you. Relax and sing well. Don't use any of the smutty jokes, though. They're OK for pubs, but not on the TV; at least not on American TV."

"You sound more like me ma every day, so you do. I'll be fine and don't wait around for me; I'll come back to the hotel with Kathleen."

Billy watched the car drive off and then walked across to where Kathleen stood smiling warmly at him. He took her arm and kissed her lightly before they walked into the building together. As the door hissed shut behind him, he saw a man wearing way too much make-up striding towards them with his hand outstretched.

"You must be Billy Murphy. Welcome to KDLP. I'm Ed Bailey. I'll be introducing you and asking you a couple of questions."

"Kathleen has given me the questions, so I hope I've got sensible answers for you."

Bailey gave an odd smile. "Good. Well, we'll see where those questions lead us, eh? Now we need to get you into make-up before the show starts."

"Make-up? Me?"

Kathleen and Bailey grinned to each other. "For TV you need to have make-up or you look like a corpse. We'll wash it off again before you go out in the daylight, never fear."

Kathleen took his arm. "Come on, Billy, I'll not let them paint you up too much, I promise."

She led him to the elevators and they rode up to the third floor. As the doors slid open she led him to the left, down a narrow corridor and into a room with what looked like a row of hairdresser's chairs. A chubby woman in a blue overall bustled across as they entered.

"Hello, dear, you're the singer are you? Never mind, sit yourself down in that one, will you, and we'll get started. You can run along, dear, I won't damage your boyfriend."

Kathleen patted his arm and left him to the tender mercies of the make-up lady, who flung a cape around him, took off his glasses and took a long look at his face. She pottered away and came back with a large tray of creams and potions as far as Billy could see.

"You've got plenty of colour in your face already, so you're not like these pasty-faced TV types, are you, dear? Makes my job a little easier and I won't have to use so much foundation to get you looking right for the camera."

She chattered away as she was working and didn't seem to need any input from him, so he sat quietly and let her get on with it. After half an hour Kathleen reappeared around the door and looked him over.

"You've made a good job of him, Ellie. He looks almost handsome."

Ellie grinned happily. "Oh, he was handsome before I started. He'll look good on the screen, won't you, dear? Now, when you're finished come back in here and I'll take it all off for you. Don't just wash it off in the bathroom or it'll run and stain your shirt. Now 'break a leg' and enjoy the show, dear."

Billy followed Kathleen back to the elevator and they went down to the studio level. She showed him to the door labelled '4' and he went inside. To the right was a control booth with a glass window and in front of him were two cameras, one facing Ed Bailey, who was already sitting there and the other facing an empty chair.

"Come on in, Billy, and take a seat. How did you find Ellie?"

"Very nice, but does she ever draw a breath? Never heard anyone talk quite so fast."

Bailey chuckled. "She is a gem, isn't she? Now then, here's how we arrange this. You sit there and that camera will focus on you. The other one will be looking at me. Dan there in the control booth will switch between them when he is editing. You will be recorded the whole time we are interviewing, so don't pick your nose. You've seen the outline script and we'll stay more or less with that. So when you are ready we'll begin."

Billy settled himself in the chair and took his guitar out of the case. "Shall I be holding this or should I put it down?"

"If you lean it there on that stand you can reach it when it's time for you to sing. We'll probably just stay with the two songs unless we get through this quickly, when I might ask you for another that we can use if we need it. Happy? OK then, as soon as Dan gives us the word we'll get going."

Dan raised his hand behind the glass of the soundproof control booth and pointed to Bailey. The interviewer nodded and turned to face Billy.

"Now then, we are joined today by Billy Murphy, all the way from Belfast, Ireland. Billy, tell us a little about what you are doing over here in the States, would you?"

Billy swallowed and then launched into the story he had rehearsed for so long with Flaherty. He settled down and the words flowed with Bailey sitting opposite him and nodding as he went along. Every now and then Bailey would interject to follow up on a point that appeared in the story. As he started to run out of steam Ed nodded to the control booth and turned back to Billy.

"Well now, Billy, we've heard about the songs you've been singing in the Irish pubs to raise money for good causes in Ireland. So now I think it's time we heard one of those songs. Do you have one you'd like to do for us? I hear 'Kevin Barry' is one of your favourites."

"So it is, Ed, and I'd love to sing it for you now."

He picked up the guitar from beside him and gave it a quick strum to check the tuning. He didn't do his tuning joke so that he could use it in the pubs as a warm-up later. His fingers found their places on the frets and he began to sing the mournful song about a young Irish hero dying for the cause. He finished it and looked up at Bailey, who had that odd smile back on his face.

"That was an interesting song there. I think our audience would agree. What do you think, Dan?"

Dan's voice came over the studio intercom. "Well now, Ed, I think we need to hear from someone who has an opinion about such songs, don't you?"

Bailey nodded and glanced at Billy. "I think you're right, Dan. Who do you have in mind?"

Billy looked between the two men. This was starting to feel uncomfortable. This wasn't in the script he had been given.

"Ed, I think this is the time to wheel in Roger Sinclair. He comes from Belfast as well, so he knows what he is talking about."

There was movement behind the glass of the control booth and Billy saw an older man with silver-grey hair come in and sit down beside the technician. The man looked through the glass with almost no expression on his face.

"This is Mr Sinclair, Billy. He was listening to your singing from the green room outside. So tell me, Roger, what's your opinion of that song?"

"The same terrorist claptrap I've been hearing all my life. Irish rebel heroes and the bold IRA. Utter drivel, the lot of it."

Bailey grinned at Billy. "So would you tell us more about that? Why do you think that way?"

Sinclair looked through the glass at Billy. "Well, maybe we could ask why Mr Murphy here doesn't sing about the bold IRA and Mick Islania? Maybe he could sing about Michael Willetts or maybe even Gary Barlow?"

Billy sat very still. He knew he had been ambushed, but had no idea where this was going. Bailey watched him and waited for a second or two before he spoke.

"So then, Billy, do you know any songs about the people Roger has named? Would you like to sing them for us?"

Billy shook his head. He could feel the sweat starting to trickle down his spine and his hands were damp.

"I don't know those people, unless he's talking about the Gary Barlow who was in a boy band. 'Take That' I think it was. Why should I know songs about them?"

"Roger?"

"I thought you must have songs about them, since all three were killed by the bold IRA you are so proud of. Maybe I should refresh your memory? Or maybe these IRA triumphs are not told to people of your age anymore?"

Bailey didn't wait for Billy to answer. "Yes. Why don't you tell us about them, Roger? Maybe that'll refresh the Minstrel Boy's memory? Then we can hear his songs about them."

Chapter 30
25ᵗʰ May 1971

Sinclair stood up behind the glass of the booth and stared fixedly at Billy. "The first one I want to talk about is Sergeant Michael Willetts. He was a member of the Parachute Regiment. He was on duty in the Springfield Road Police Station in Belfast. He was there to provide extra security because there had been trouble in the area recently. He was in the entrance lobby watching the people come in who had business with the police. He was chatting with them to keep things lightweight and calm. Then one of your IRA friends threw a suitcase bomb in through the door and ran like hell. Willetts saw the bomb and saw that a woman and her two children were in danger. He shepherded them away from the bomb and shielded them with his own body.

"The bomb exploded and shrapnel was blasted all over. A piece of a metal locker was blown across the room and struck the Sergeant in the back. He died at the scene, but the woman and her two children were safe. Two other soldiers and eighteen civilians were injured by this brave act by the IRA.

"As Willetts' body and the injured were carried out they were jeered by a mob of youths in the street. So come on, Murphy, give us a song about the bravery of the IRA."

Billy sat very still and said nothing. He looked at Sinclair, who nodded back at him.
4ᵗʰ March 1973

"Fair enough then, if you don't know that triumphant song, how about Private Gary Barlow? He was part of a team searching for weapons in the Divis Flats in Belfast. The army wanted to get the arms out of the hands of the terrorists so they could not be used to kill more innocent civilians. At the end of the search the army pulled out, but a mistake was made and Gary was left behind, on his own. He had no idea the rest of his patrol had gone.

"In short order he was surrounded by a large group of women who started to force him backwards. Now you should remember this young soldier was armed; he could have shot his way out of there, but he didn't. He was an honourable young man and the British Army doesn't shoot unarmed women, which is a lot more then you can say for your heroic IRA. Anyway, this mob of harridans forced him backwards into a garage. They kept him trapped there and at some point his rifle was dragged out of his hands. They forced him to stay and then sent for a murderer. One of your bold IRA volunteers was called to the garage and murdered a decent young man for the crime of being decent and not shooting women to save his own life. He was just nineteen years old and he didn't deserve that.

"Have you got a song about that one then, Billy? Come on, give us a tune."

26th October 1989

Sinclair took a sip of water from the glass on the desk in front of him. "I suppose you won't have a song about the next one, but maybe it's difficult to find a rhyme for Islania?

"Corporal Mick Islania was in the Royal Air Force and stationed in Germany. He was a communications technician. He fixed the radios on the aircraft that were deployed there as part of the NATO forces that protected Western Europe, including Ireland. He had never served in Ulster. His car stopped in a garage to fill up before driving home. His wife was in the driving seat.

"Two of your heroic 'freedom fighters' stepped up to the car carrying AK47 automatic rifles and opened fire. The Corporal was slaughtered where he sat, alongside his wife. There's a fine photograph of his funeral on the internet, if you are interested. His coffin is being carried shoulder-high by six of his RAF comrades. Of course behind them is another one of his friends, carrying a very small white coffin in his arms. His six-month-old daughter was also shot to death in the car. His wife, Smita, was cradling her dead child when help got to her.

"So now then, Mr Murphy, why don't you justify those killings as part of your armed struggle? Young men trying to keep people safe and a six-month-old baby girl. What the hell had she ever done to justify murdering her?"

Billy stood up slowly, still holding the guitar. He looked through the glass at Sinclair and then at Bailey, who sat silently watching him. He shook his head and walked out of the room. He walked along the corridor to the stairway and then went down and out of the front door.

Chapter 31

He was still shaking as he climbed out of the taxi and walked back into the hotel. He turned left after the lobby and went into the corner bar. As he expected, Flaherty was sitting behind a beer at a table by the wall. He walked over and sat down with a sigh.

"You know you've still got make-up on, Billy?"

He wiped a finger along his cheek and looked at the powder. "It was a disaster, Paddy. I was bloody ambushed. The studio was a set-up. They had some Brit there who trotted out a list of the mistakes that were made during the Troubles. He made it sound as though the IRA was off the leash and didn't give a shit who they killed or why."

"Ye feckin eejit! Whenever you get into that kind of situation just throw Bloody Sunday in their teeth!"

"And how the bloody hell was I supposed to know that?"

"Ah Christ! It's bloody obvious! You throw them off with the major army fuck-up of the whole of the Troubles."

"It may be bloody obvious to you, but that was all before I was born, for heaven's sake. I know next to bugger all about it."

The two stared at each other, both flushed and angry. Then Flaherty sighed and slumped back in his chair. He looked up at the ceiling high above them and swore quietly.

Then he spoke quietly and calmly. "Probably my fault for not warning you. What incidents did they bring up then?"

Billy sat back and looked up at the ceiling. "There was someone called Islania and his daughter. She was only six months old, for Christ's sake. Then there was Gary Barlow and Michael Willetts, both soldiers."

"Islania was a major cock-up, that's for sure. O'Shea did that one, the mad bastard. Barlow was a legitimate target, but the way it was done handed the Brits a PR gift. That one was bloody O'Shea as well. Bloody Willetts was a hero, right enough, but we couldn't predict he would do that. Was that all?"

"Wasn't that enough? It made me look like a right shit, so it did."

"What did you do?"

"I walked out. What the hell else could I do? I can't believe Kathleen set me up this way. I thought she liked me."

Flaherty gazed across the room and through the window. "Maybe she didn't know? Maybe the studio saw an opportunity to make trouble that would get their station noticed by the big networks? Don't get angry with her when she comes back. Explain what happened and see if she can get the tape for us. We might be able to stop it getting broadcast."

Billy smiled slightly. "I don't think there's any tapes involved. That studio seemed to have modern digital equipment."

"What difference does that make? We'll get the recording wiped or whatever they do."

"I can try and maybe so can she, but with the recording being digital they can edit it so much faster. They could have it put together in no time at all and then get it out across the country."

"Damn! The wonders of modern technology, eh? Just means we'll have to get it destroyed more quickly. Can you phone the girl and see what her situation is? If she's still at the TV station she might go and do it now, before they edit it."

Billy shook his head. "I'm not sure I can talk to her after this. I might end up swearing at her and then she'll do nothing for us."

Flaherty leaned forward and poked his finger into Billy's chest. "Listen to me, you arsehole. We have to stop that being broadcast; it could do the cause a lot of damage if they edit it against us. Christ, they could even drop in some video clips. So you grow the hell up and pull yerself together. Get on the phone to that lass. If she's sweet on you then she might save our bacon. If she doesn't, then I'm going to have to do some fancy footwork to keep the boys from nailing our arses to the floor."

Chapter 32

He watched as she came across the atrium floor towards him. She was flushed and obviously upset, but he didn't move to meet her. He had no idea how to deal with this, so let her speak first.

"Billy, I am so sorry. I had no idea they were going to do that. I don't know what they were thinking of, setting you up like that."

He looked at her as calmly as he was able. "Have to give it to them, though; it was a damn fine ambush."

"I mean it, Billy, I had no idea. I know you wouldn't support any of that kind of thing, would you? I told them they'd got it all wrong. I told them you were collecting welfare funds to help people back in Ireland. I promised him Sinclair was making it up. I've been talking to Ed Bailey ever since, trying to get him to drop it, but he won't. He thinks it will make wonderful TV and get played coast to coast on the small affiliated stations. He's hoping the big networks pick it up and then he'll be made."

"Made?"

"He doesn't want to stay on a small local TV station. He wants to be noticed and be offered a job by one of the big national networks. He's ambitious and thinks this could be the thing that makes his reputation."

"Flaherty is spitting teeth about this. So how do we stop it being broadcast? Who makes the final decision on it?"

She was calming down now and her cheeks were returning to their normal colour. "It's Ed Bailey's call."

"No, I mean who is his boss? Who can override him and get this thing canned? Maybe the station owner or the manager?"

She shook her head and he watched her lovely hair swing. "You don't understand. Ed Bailey owns half the station. He doesn't have a boss. He married a rich wife and she bought him the controlling interest in the station, so he has the final say."

"Well, we'll just have to persuade him that broadcasting it is not a good idea. You stay here and I'll go up and have a word with Flaherty. He knows some people who might influence Ed."

"What do you mean influence?"

"We were speaking with a big industrialist yesterday about me singing at his daughter's birthday party. He was a nice guy and obviously loaded. If he asks Ed nicely then maybe he'll drop this story in return for a bigger one later. Let me go talk to Paddy and see if he agrees."

She stayed sitting in the green metal chair and watched him cross to the elevator. As it rose to the third floor, she saw him raise his hand and give her a small wave through its glass side. He walked along the open balcony around the atrium and she could just see him waiting at the door of Flaherty's room. He was back out in five minutes and walking towards the elevator. She thought he looked happier as he dropped down to the atrium floor and walked across towards her.

"What did he say?"

"He's still not a happy camper, but he's going to have a word with our friend to see if he can persuade Bailey not to damage us like this. He's going to explain how our fundraising is so valuable to our people back home."

"Does he think it'll work? It really is very important to Ed and he wouldn't listen to me at all."

"Lovely as you are, Kathleen, you're not rich and influential. He thinks our friend can get Bailey's attention. Now, shall we forget all this for a while and take a walk over to that big shopping mall across the way? I can treat you to an elegant lunch in the food court there."

She smiled at him, so relieved that he wasn't angry with her. "I don't know about elegant, but they will probably have Chinese food there. Let's go and see."

Chapter 33

He woke with a start as the room door crashed back on its hinges. He rolled off the bed and grabbed his glasses before walking through into the sitting room of the suite. Kathleen stood in the doorway, one arm outstretched holding the door open.

"What the hell are you people? I can't believe I've slept with you. You're bloody animals, the pair of you."

"Whoa! Slow down there. What's happened?"

"You know damn fine what's happened. Don't you play the wide-eyed innocent with me."

"Tell me."

She took a long shuddering breath. "One of your friends went to see Ed Bailey and told him to delete the interview. Ed refused and the man left. An hour later as Ed was driving out of the parking structure the same man stepped out in front of him. He didn't say anything he just raised a gun and put a bullet through the centre of the windscreen. Then he walked away, leaving Ed in shock in the car. He still had glass fragments in his hair when he was talking to me."

"Why was he talking to you?"

"I went back to try and persuade him to drop the interview. He was in his office shaking. He'd been crying. He was bloody terrified."

"Kathleen, I swear it was nothing to do with me. I've been here all day. You must know I wouldn't do that."

She let the door swing closed as she walked into the room and picked up her suitcase. She didn't look at him as she started to pack her clothes away. He stepped forward and touched her on the shoulder.

She spun away from him and snarled. "Don't you touch me! I thought Sinclair was lying or exaggerating, but it's for real. You people really are terrorists."

"Not me, Kathleen. I'm just a singer. I ..."

"Don't you give me that crap. You're raising money for them and that makes you one of them. I'm leaving and don't you come near me. I want nothing more to do with you. I'm going back to Boston and I never want to hear your name again."

"But Kathleen, we ..."

She slammed the case shut and looked at him with a deep anger in her eyes. "But Kathleen nothing! I believed in you. I brought friends to see you sing. I told people to come to your gigs and now I find out what you really are."

She picked the case up and stormed out of the room. He followed her to the doorway and watched her walk along the wide balcony towards the elevator. She never looked back. As she vanished from his sight he turned away and walked along to Flaherty's room. He knocked and waited. Flaherty opened the door and Billy walked in.

"What the hell have you done?"

Flaherty smiled. "And hello to yourself, Billy boy. Now what troubles you?"

"Kathleen has left me. Some damned fool went and tried to get Bailey to drop the interview.

When he wouldn't he shot through the windscreen of his car. Was that your doing?"

"Ah, I see why you're upset. I should have told you. It wasn't my doing as such. I told Mulgrew to make sure Bailey agreed, but I told him not to kill him, I promise."

"He shot at him, for Christ's sake. Bailey is just lucky that he missed."

"He didn't miss. The Mulgrew is a fancy shot with a pistol and a rifle. He was a sniper back in the day. If he had wanted to hit Bailey he would be on a mortuary slab by now. No, that was just a warning to do as he's been told or worse could be coming."

"I thought you said we were going to persuade him to drop it?"

Flaherty chuckled and sat down. "And do you not think that he might be persuaded now? He's had a clear warning of consequences."

"Oh yes, and when the police come banging down our door? What then?"

"Sure and we've been here all day have we not? Sit down and calm yourself. We've been doing this sort of thing for years, we know what works. If Bailey has any sense, he'll go home and change his underwear before he deletes the interview and nothing will be said to any police. Now get the coffee on and calm yourself, boy. It's all over and the boys back home won't need to send anyone to deal with us."

Billy's shoulders sagged. "And what am I supposed to do about Kathleen?"

"That ship has sailed, boy, and a good thing too. Forget about her and move on."

Billy walked across the room to the small kitchenette. He busied himself making the coffee in the hotel-supplied percolator. As it bubbled and spat the hot water into the filter he walked back and sat down on the other chair.

"So who the hell is Mulgrew anyway?"

"Fergus Mulgrew is a Derry man. He was one of our best snipers during the armed struggle. We used him all over the province for the special jobs when we really wanted to send a message."

"So why is he here in Seattle?"

"As well as being here to help us with making contacts you mean? Same as the others you've met. Things got too hot for him in Ireland and he needed a place where the British wouldn't find him so easily. There's quite a few of the volunteers that moved out of Ireland as things started to slow down. We got intelligence that the army and the police were looking for some payback and they weren't going to play by the rules to get it."

"The rules? What rules are they?"

"The British government wouldn't let them take the gloves off. Every one of them was issued with this damn silly little card that told them when they could open fire and the warnings they had to shout. If they fired and the Military Police found they hadn't followed the card they were in the shit. It tied one hand behind their backs for the whole time we were fighting them. Anyway, when the Good Friday Agreement was coming through we heard that some of them didn't agree and were going to freelance to get their own back. Maybe that's what this AVNI thing is."

Billy stood and went across to the coffee pot. He didn't speak until he was back with the two mugs of black coffee. He put one down in front of Flaherty and returned to his chair.

"So what now then?"

Flaherty sipped the strong brew and sighed in satisfaction. "For hotel coffee this Embassy Suites stuff isn't too bad. Anyway, Mulgrew is coming to see me anytime now. You might as well meet him and hear what he has to say. He was trying to arrange us some gigs down around Pioneer Square in Seattle itself."

Billy put his mug down next to the chair. "I thought we weren't supposed to meet him? If one of these AVNI maniacs is watching us he could spot Mulgrew coming here."

Flaherty nodded and smiled. "Ah now you're thinking the right way, boy. Mulgrew is going to check in as a guest so he looks legit. He'll call from his room and we leave the door on the latch. He'll just slip in with nobody the wiser."

Chapter 34

The ringing of the phone by the bedside woke Billy from a troubled sleep. The bed felt big and empty without Kathleen and he was devastated to have lost her this way. He rolled over and picked up the handset, knocking his glasses to the floor as he did so.

"What?"

He heard Flaherty's voice. "Billy, come along to my room now. There's someone for you to meet."

He swore quietly to himself as he dressed and then fumbled about on the floor until he found the glasses. He walked through to the door and checked around before stepping outside. The hotel was deserted and silent at this time of the morning as he walked along to Flaherty's room. The door was slightly open and he pushed it wide before walking in.

Flaherty and a small man were sitting in the two chairs as he closed the door behind them. Billy didn't offer to shake hands as he dropped himself onto the sofa.

"Fergus, this is Billy, our Minstrel Boy, and a fine cover he is making for the real fundraising. Billy say hello to Fergus."

Billy nodded at the newcomer. "Fergus. I'd like to say it's nice to meet you, but at two in the morning it really isn't."

The small man had a pronounced Derry accent as he spoke quietly. "You'll need to be getting used to the strange hours for when the armed struggle kicks back into high gear, boy."

Billy shook his head. "That stuff is not for me. I'm just a singer and I'll help raise the funds, but that's it."

Mulgrew smiled slightly and leaned back in the chair. "You'll do as you're feckin told. If the boys tell you to carry a bomb or transport weapons, you'll do it if you value your knees. A 9mm round through the kneecap is something you want to avoid, I promise you."

Billy tried not to look nervous as he looked across to Flaherty. "So did you drag me out of bed just to threaten me or is there something else?"

Flaherty didn't smile. "Watch your mouth there, Billy. This is a serious business and you don't want to be taking it lightly."

"Fine. What do you want of me?"

"Over to you, Mulgrew. Tell us what you have planned for us."

Mulgrew sat up and leaned forward. "Right then, I've got four Irish bars for you to do your singing routine in. I've got the list here with the name of the contact to deal with in each one. The most important booking, though, is the Saturday afternoon when our minstrel here sings for the birthday party. While he's doing that, you and me can go and sit down with our contact and finalise the details for the big funding input."

"Why are you part of that discussion, Fergus? I thought it would be just me."

"Not so. The boys want me to be there so there is a witness that everything is on the up and up. Plus of course, they want our new friend to know me so that, if I need to speak to him to keep him on the narrow path, he'll know it comes from the boys in Belfast."

"I can't see him playing fast and loose with us; he has an awful lot to gain when we take over, so he does."

"Ach, that's true enough, but these Americans have always got the eye out for the main chance. If he thinks he can gain something by shitting on us, he might be tempted. So I'm to be here as a small warning voice on his shoulder, until everything has gone through the way we want."

"And will you be taking a bribe as well?" Billy asked.

The small man turned his head very slowly to look at the young singer. "And what business of yours would that be? If he offers me a gratuity for helping him then why would I refuse?"

There was something in the eyes and the voice that made Billy shut his mouth and sit very still. He felt he could reach out and touch the menace in the room and the cold sweat trickled down his spine.

Flaherty saw the look on Billy's face and nodded to Mulgrew. "That should be all we need with Billy. We'll meet up in the atrium for breakfast and we can discuss any details that we think of then. Sleep well, Billy boy, and try not to miss the lovely Kathleen."

Chapter 35

As he leaned on the balcony wall outside his room he could see down into the massive atrium where breakfast was being served. Flaherty sat at his usual table away from most of the other guests, apparently deep in conversation with Mulgrew. He considered going back into his room and giving it a miss, but the call of the omelettes and bacon was too much and he braced himself for the unpleasant local contact.

Flaherty saw him as he dropped downwards in the glass lift and raised a hand in greeting. He walked across and ordered his breakfast from the sweating chef and then went to fill his coffee mug. He picked up his order and walked to the table where the others sat.

"Did you sleep well enough then, Billy boy? Even without the fair Kathleen to rock your world?"

He cut a piece of the omelette. "I slept fine well, thank you for asking, even with being woken up in the middle of the night to be threatened."

Mulgrew chuckled, but there was no humour in the sound. "You're far too sensitive, boy. A real threat is when the pistol barrel is resting on your kneecap and I give you a few seconds to beg me not to fire. I always enjoy that part. The sweating and the promising. Never gets old for me."

Billy put down his fork. "You really are a bastard, aren't you?"

The small man smiled. "That I am, but a man has to find his entertainment where he can. For now, I've had enough. I'll leave you to eat your breakfast in peace."

They watched as he walked away, then Flaherty cleared his throat. "You should be careful what you say to the Mulgrew, Billy. He's a nasty piece of work and a stone-cold killer, so he is. Not sure if he's a psychopath or a sociopath, but he's not right in the head for sure."

Billy picked up his fork again and sliced into the eggs. "Then why the hell do we have to deal with him?"

"If you are going to have an armed struggle again, and we are, then a killer like that is a useful tool to have. Point him at a target and turn him loose. That's what we did in South Armagh and he was damned effective. 'One shot, one kill' they called him and the British never came close to catching him. By the time they recovered from the shock, him and his spotter were long gone."

"So what targets did you point him at?"

"The favourites were soldiers who were foot patrolling round the streets. He'd drop one and be gone. Then the locals could sit behind their windows and watch the soldiers running round trying to save the target and find the sniper. Better than a show on the TV it was."

"What the hell was the point in killing a man for patrolling the streets?"

"Demoralisation, boy. Make them feel bad, increase the fear and have them looking over their shoulder all the time. Same basic idea now as we try and get the old soldiers prosecuted for shooting people, even though most of them were returning fire. Demoralisation will slow them down when we start the armed struggle again. Make them slow to react. Make them second-guess everything and while they are doing that we sweep to power and take over the whole island. This is nearly our time and the British and the Protestants won't know what hit them."

"So shooting these men was what got him hiding over here then?"

"That's right. If the army could find him he'd be in trouble for sure. He made their lives a misery down in the border country. Hell, sometimes he fired from inside the Republic where he knew they couldn't follow him. Made life easy, that did, and the Garda were always slow to follow up, so he could just walk away."

Chapter 36
2nd December 1993

Mulgrew settled behind the large black rifle on the high ground by the Granemore Road. The position was perfect and the outlying scout had already called on the radio that a patrol was moving into the target area. Next to him his primary spotter scanned the area through powerful binoculars. He adjusted the telescopic sight on top of the .50 Barrett rifle and made sure the bipod legs were firmly placed. It was still and cold as usual for December in South Armagh, with rain forecast to move in from the Atlantic later.

He had chosen where the patrol would be when he took the shot. They tried to vary their routes, but there was not much choice for them in this area of Keady. He would choose his mark and take him as he went past Lir Gardens. He lowered his head to the sight and took a look at the target area. There were kids in the street, but they would not bother him. If one of them got hit the IRA would find a way to blame the army, the way they always did. The locals would know it was bullshit, but they would say nothing and would mount a demonstration against the army if they were ordered to. They had no choice if they wanted to keep their kneecaps intact.

He saw movement and swung the rifle a few millimetres to the left to take a look. The patrol was here. Through the sight he could see they looked exhausted. That was good; it would slow them down and one of them was going to have a long, long sleep anytime now.

He looked across to his spotter. "Which one do you want?"

His companion grinned. "Why not take the darkie at the back? We haven't dropped a black one for a while."

Mulgrew returned his eye to the sight and started to control his breathing. "Black one, it is. I've got him now. You move out and make sure Sean has the car ready to move. Open up the trunk so I can drop the rifle in. We need to be away quick from this one."

The spotter wriggled backwards making sure he didn't show above the skyline while Mulgrew continued to watch the patrol. They may be tired, but they were still alert. He could see their heads tracking left and right as they looked for any threat. They weren't looking this far out, though. He smiled; this was going to be an easy one.

The patrol continued to move forward and the man they had selected moved into the killing area. He was the last man, the tail end Charlie, as they were sometimes called. Through the optics he could see the whites of his eyes against his dark skin. Two more paces and you're mine, he thought. The soldier turned and looked behind to make sure there was no threat to his comrades from that direction as Mulgrew stopped his breathing and gently squeezed the trigger.

The powerful rifle bucked upwards and backwards against his shoulder and he saw the target crash to the ground with a scream that he could hear all the way out here. He pulled back and slithered down the slight slope behind him. Once he was behind the small ridge he got to his feet and trotted to the waiting car. The rifle went into the trunk and the wheels were spinning before he got the door shut.

Behind them Lance Bombardier Paul Garrett lay on the ground with a massive wound to his stomach. The local doctor and a nurse ran to help him while his stunned patrol secured the area and called for backup. Despite the desperate attempts to stop the bleeding, he died in the gutter of the town he was trying to protect, six minutes after being shot.

Billy sat quite still at the end of Flaherty's story. "So how do you know all the details?"

"Sure and I was the scout that day. I stood in the street and watched it all play out. Mulgrew told me the details of his part in the pub later when we were celebrating."

12th February 1997

"Then there was the one where he really had to leave the province if he wanted to stay alive. That one was in '97. The peace process was rolling forward and although there was no official ceasefire in place the IRA army council had given orders we weren't to shoot anyone unless we had to. But that mad bastard Mulgrew wanted another one and his team were more scared of him than they were of the army council, so they went along with it.

149

"The army had set up a vehicle checkpoint and were stopping cars as they went through. Making sure that none of the real players were on the move. They were fairly relaxed as they knew the peace process was nearly done, as did everyone else. So anyway, this young lad was on the roadside and he was speaking to the driver, a young Catholic woman. They were just chatting and he was handing her back her driving licence when Mulgrew let rip. She said later that he had been smiling at her when the bullet hit him. He was hit in the back and, with it being a Barrett rifle, the round went straight through him. It hardly even hardly slowed down with his body armour. The woman in the car was sprayed with his blood and the round skimmed across her forehead. Really lucky he didn't kill her or Mulgrew would have been a dead man walking.

"Either way there was a hell of a fuss from both communities. They knew peace was almost here and they knew there was no reason to kill the boy. Plus of course, the army council had passed the word to hold back. It may even have pushed the peace process along a bit and over the last hump.

"In any case the young lad was Lance Bombardier Stephen Restorick, and he was the last one the IRA killed during the armed struggle. Well, officially, that is. We did have a little bit of tidying up to do later."

"And what of Mulgrew?"

"Ah, he was told to get the fuck out of Ireland if he wanted to survive. There were volunteers who wanted him dead, as well as the British army. He disobeyed an order, you see, and we can't have that, so we can't."

"So he really is a murdering bastard then?"

"Like I said, he's not right in the head. He kills for fun and he does the kneecappings with a big fat smile on his weasel face as well."

Chapter 37

The gravel crunched below their wheels as they drove up to the impressive house set back in the wooded country behind Seattle. Billy stood open-mouthed as he got out and looked around him. He recovered as Flaherty slapped his arm.

"Get your guitar out and hurry up. We're late and the party is due to start in about half an hour."

They walked to the front of the house as the taxi drove away and Flaherty used the ornate brass knocker on the highly polished wooden door. The doors swung open almost immediately and a tall man looked them up and down with a quizzical expression on his face.

"Are you guests, gentlemen?"

"In a manner of speaking. I'm here to speak to the boss and Billy here is going to sing some songs at the party, so he is."

"I see. In which case would you care to walk around that side of the house and you will find the party organiser. She can show you where to set up. I will advise my employer that you are here if I might have your name? Perhaps you will go around and wait in the garden too. I will come for you when he is able to speak to you."

Billy smiled secretly to himself as he saw Flaherty's expression. The older man had obviously expected a better reception. They walked together around the house until they found a harassed woman in a white dress who was issuing instructions to the caterers.

Flaherty was still unhappy, so Billy spoke to her. "Hello there. I guess you must be organising this bunfight. I'm the singer they've ordered."

She turned irritated eyes to him and sniffed. "Which one are you? They have a number of musical events to be set up in the garden."

He smiled. "I'm Billy Murphy, I sing lilting Irish songs to charm the birds from the trees and to woo lovely ladies such as yerself."

Her eyes softened and she gave him a small smile. "Ah yes. The guitar player. You're down by the barbecue pit over there."

Billy looked across the extensive grounds that stretched to the forest edge. "Sorry, where would that be?"

"Come on, I'll walk you down. I need a break from these damned caterers anyway. They're supposed to be professionals, but you'd never know it."

They walked across the wide sloping lawn towards a wooden-roofed pergola that sat next to a depression that looked like a golf bunker. The man dressed in chef's whites was preparing food and getting the large barbecue to the right temperature.

"You set yourself up under the pergola. The guests will probably come there to eat their burgers and such, to get a little shade. While it's quiet keep an eye on the treeline. There's an old black bear that wanders through here sometimes. She won't come by once all the people arrive."

"Are you serious or is that a joke?"

She looked surprised. "Why would I joke? There are bears all over these forests, though they usually stay clear of people."

"Right you are then. When do you want me to start playing?"

"The rock band is way over there, so that's the noisy end. No point you trying to compete with them, so just start playing when the people who want barbecue food start to drift over here."

Billy nodded and took his guitar out of its case. "I'll be fine here. Will I see you later?"

The smile was broader this time. "I'll probably drop by to see how you are doing once I have everything set up and running."

"I'll look forward to that then."

He watched her walk away back up the slope and then glanced at the silent Flaherty. "Looks like the boss wants to see you now. The flunkey from the front door is over there and looking around."

Flaherty looked up the slope just as the man saw him and waved his arm. "I'll see you later, Billy. No idea how long this will take."

"Take your time. I'm going to see if I can get a burger or something before this all kicks off."

As Flaherty walked away, Billy put his guitar down carefully and walked to the barbecue pit to speak to the chef. "Hello there, I'm Billy. I'm the singer, so it looks like you and me are a double act."

The sweating man looked up from the coals and wiped his hand on a small towel. "Ernesto. You worked for these people before?"

"No, never. Are they OK?"

Ernesto shrugged. "The daughter is nice enough, but the old man and her mother are sons of bitches. Seems they have a speech impediment; they can't say please and they can't say thank you."

"Maybe that's just part of being rich?"

"No way. I work at lots of the big houses round here and they are all nice to me except these ones. Still, I need the money, so I work where I can."

"Will many people come down here for the barbecue with all the other things available?"

"Sometimes. It depends where Caroline goes. She is the daughter. Very pretty girl with lots of pretty girlfriends. If she comes here with her friends then the boys will follow them like panting sheepdogs."

Billy sat down on the bank at the edge of the pit and looked around him. "I've never seen a place like this back home. Is it true there are bears in the forest?"

Ernesto chuckled. "Oh yes, lots of them, but they won't come here if there are a lot of people. They are sensible creatures."

"Are they dangerous?"

"Dangerous? Sometimes if they are hungry or if you corner them, then yes. If you get between them and their cubs they are really angry. You know how to tell the difference between a black bear and grizzly?"

Billy shook his head. "No, how?"

"Easy: if the bear is chasing you then you climb a tree. If it's a black bear it will climb after you. If it's a grizzly it just knocks the tree down."

Ernesto chuckled at Billy's shocked expression. "Is a joke. You want something to eat before the guests arrive?"

"You got burgers?"

"You make a joke with me now, eh? I have everything, burgers, steaks, ribs and chickens."

"Can I take just a burger, please?"

"Just a burger? I don't do just a burger. I make the best burgers on the Pacific coast. You wait until you taste it and tell me if I lie."

Chapter 38

The burger was all that Ernesto had promised and he was finishing it and wiping the grease off his fingers when he saw a group of young women heading towards him down the sloping lawn. He walked back over to the pergola and picked up his guitar. He strummed a little to check the tuning as they reached him.

"Are you the Irish singer?"

"That's me, fair colleen, and who would you be?"

She tossed her long blonde hair to one side and looked him in the eye. "I'm Caroline. It's my birthday party."

"Caroline, the chef here is a liar. He just said you were pretty and you're way past that."

She smiled broadly and giggled. "I think I like you already. So what are you going to sing for us?"

"Anything your heart desires, or would you like to just let me ramble through some songs for you?"

"Just ramble."

"I'll do that, but I need you and your friends to sing the chorus with me or my songs don't work. Is that a deal?"

She glanced around at her friends and they all nodded. "We need some drinks from the barbecue man and then we'll sing with you."

He sang them the easy ones which had the best chorus and in minutes he had them eating out of his hand. As he played he saw the young men following down the hill and the girls shook their heads and grinned at each other. Caroline made them join in with the singing and in a short while they were enjoying it too. He sang until Caroline stood up and walked up to him.

He held the guitar as she spoke. "I'm sorry, Billy, I'll have to go and circulate or my dad will get mad. Will you still be here later? I'd like to hear some more."

As she walked away her entourage followed her and he sat quietly watching them go. Flaherty passed them as he walked down the lawn towards the pergola.

"So how did it go with the big boss then, Paddy?"

Flaherty tapped his breast pocket. "Better than we expected. I've got a banker's draft in here and it's a big one."

"And how about the gratuity for you and Mulgrew? You get that, did you?"

"The Mulgrew didn't bother to turn up, so to hell with him. You can have what he thought he was going to get."

Flaherty pulled a white envelope out of an inside pocket and handed it over. Billy flipped it open and looked at the wad of bank notes inside.

"You want me to have all this?"

"You've had a couple of rough goes that you didn't deserve, Billy boy, so that's my way of apologising properly. You've kept up your end of the bargain better than I have."

"What about Mulgrew? Isn't he going to want his piece of the action?"

"If he can't be bothered to turn up then he gets nothing. We'll see him right later on. Now, how about we push off out of here and get back to Seattle?"

Billy shook his head. "Can't do that. The birthday girl wants me to stay and sing to her some more."

"Fair go. We don't want her complaining to her daddy. Is the food here any good?"

"Talk to Ernesto down there, he makes a truly fine burger."

***

It was dark by the time they made it back to the Embassy Suites in Tacoma and Billy was half asleep in the back seat. Flaherty nudged him as the car pulled in to the front of the hotel. They walked in and decided to give the bar a miss. The two of them rode the elevator to the third floor and walked along the balcony.

"I'm away to call on our absent friend, to see what the devil he's playing at. I'll see you in the morning."

Billy closed the door and set the guitar down on the table. He dropped his jacket on the chair and headed for the bedroom area to undress and get a shower. He stopped as the rapid knocking came on the door. He walked back and pulled it open to let Flaherty in.

The older man was pale and sweating. "It's happened again."

"What has?"

"What the hell do you imagine? Mulgrew is dead. Spark out on the floor of his room with blood all over the place."

"Are you sure he's dead? Shouldn't we call 911?"

"The two holes in his face and the back of his skull that's been blown off are pretty feckin convincing, but if you want to give him the kiss of life be my bloody guest."

Billy sat down heavily. "Oh Christ. Does that mean they'll be after us next?"

"God only knows. Now get off your arse and come and help me."

"Do what?"

"We need to wipe down to get rid of any of our fingerprints, and then we need to check he's left nothing behind that could point to us."

"Right now?"

"Yes now. We need to be pure as the driven snow when the coppers get here. If they connect this to the killings in Boston and New York we could be in deep shit."

"Then what do we do? Do we just sit here and play the innocents?"

"No, we get the hell out of here. The plan was always to do Australia next, so we're going to bring that forward. Now get a damned move on."

They walked quickly along the balcony and went into the room after checking they were not being observed. Billy gagged a little as they went inside. He could hardly believe there had been so much blood inside such a small man. Flaherty closed the door and switched the overhead light on. The blood was splattered across the furniture and up the walls. There were deep red, almost black, pools soaking into the carpet below the body and Billy gagged again when he saw the grey brain matter that dripped slowly down the front of the armchair that Mulgrew had sat in the last time he was in this room.

The blood smears across the floor showed that Mulgrew had not died immediately. The blood that made the marks had come from the holes through his kneecaps and another through the palm of his right hand. The two bullets to the face had finished him off and blown the back of his head across the room.

"Dear Lord. Who would do this?"

"I told you, Billy, the army wanted this bastard badly. He made their lives a misery for a long time and they know about the kneecappings, it seems."

"No sign of the AVNI card this time, though."

Flaherty reached into his pocket and drew out the bloodstained card. "I already took it so the cops won't link it back to the others. We're being hunted, Billy, so now you wipe for fingerprints and check for any papers, and for Christ's sake make sure you don't track your footprints through the blood. I'm going down to the lobby to book a flight to get us the hell out of here and away."

Chapter 39

He checked his watch as the brakes released and he was pressed back in his seat as the aircraft accelerated along the runway. Hawaiian Airlines, Flight HA21 was leaving SeaTac airport right on time. In six hours they would be in Honolulu and fifty minutes after that they would be on the way to Sydney in Australia. The eleven-hour flight across the Pacific was going to be a trial in these economy seats, but Flaherty had insisted on saving money. The early flight ensured they would be in the air before the body was discovered and awkward questions were asked.

The extremely attractive stewardess moved slowly through the cabin once the seat belt sign was turned off. Flaherty ordered a whiskey as she reached him and lay back in the seat to drink it. Billy gave her a smile but didn't order anything.

"Bit early for the hard stuff, isn't it?"

"Billy, son, I've got six hours in this seat and if I'm going to catch up on the sleep I missed last night I'll need a calmer. You should try it."

"I'll manage, thank you. What the hell are we going to do in Sydney? They won't be ready for us, so we'll just be hanging around."

Flaherty sipped again and smiled. "All set up, boy, never fear. Our contact will be waiting for us at the airport and we'll be away before anybody can spot us. No hotels this time. Too easy to track us. We're going to keep our heads down while the boys at home try and work out who these AVNI bastards are and what to do about them."

"I'd have thought that was blindingly obvious."

"Kill them, you mean? Not our call, my son. We are on a ceasefire, remember? So we let the senior council members decide and then they'll send someone, if that's the decision."

"I thought we were going to be working with industrialists in the States to raise the serious money? So now what do we do?"

"Not all Australians walk round in hats with corks dangling off them. They have serious people who want to make big money as well. Once we get the word we'll be talking to them and then we'll be heading back to the US to pick up where we left off. It's all in hand, Billy boy. Now try and get some beauty sleep. You look like hell."

***

Eighteen hours after leaving Seattle the aircraft touched down in Sydney and they blundered through the customs formalities in a daze. As they dragged their baggage out of the customs hall Flaherty stopped and gripped the hand of the man who stood grinning at them.

"Billy, come you here and meet a living legend."

Billy walked across and took the outstretched hand. "Billy, this is Eoin Cleary, the man who made England shake."

"You're a musician then?"

Eoin laughed. "No, son, my music was with the gelignite and I played a tune all over England."

Flaherty slapped Billy on the back. "Eoin was the bomb maker for one of our active service

163

units operating on the mainland. He's got some tales to tell when we get settled."

"Come on, the both of you, the car is just across the way and we've got a couple of hours before we get home. Don't want to hang around here and get spotted by whoever is monitoring you."

They walked after their contact. "So you think we are being monitored then?"

"I've no idea, Paddy, but that's what the boys in Belfast think. The killings that are following you are too much of a coincidence. They've told me to be damned careful as well. They reckon if the people out for revenge have a list then I'll be on it."

"They have any idea who it is yet?"

"Here's the car. Throw your bags in the back. The latest thinking is that it's some ex-army people out for revenge or maybe they are trying to send a message about the PSNI hunting down their old comrades. Couldn't blame them for that. It's going well, I hear?"

Flaherty fastened his seat belt. "It is. Our people at the top of the police have got a list of the ones we want to go after. All pensioners now, of course, and the British government is throwing them to the wolves. Lots of fine words in Parliament about supporting their veterans, but they do nothing, the spineless bastards."

"And is it working?"

Flaherty leaned back and sighed. "It seems to be. They can't recruit enough people to fill the army. Maybe the potential recruits can see that, with no backing, any action they take could result in them being hounded for life. And the best part is that the British taxpayer is funding these prosecutions for us. You couldn't make it up."

As they cleared the city and drove along the wide smooth road, the tiredness got the better of them and Flaherty and Billy slept. They woke as the car pulled up outside a white bungalow with a wide veranda at the front.

"Home sweet home, lads. Far enough from the city not to be noticed, but close enough to drive in and get whatever we need."

Billy climbed out of the back door of the car and stretched his stiff muscles. He looked around in the gathering dark at the trees that surrounded the house. The track they must have come down snaked away into the woodland and disappeared after a couple of hundred metres.

"No near neighbours, Billy, if that's what you're looking for. We're on a nice big plot here and once we're settled I'll let the dogs out. Nobody is going to be sneaking up on us, I promise you that."

Billy took his battered guitar case out of the car. "Good to hear. So how long are we staying here?"

Eoin grabbed one of the bags and started to walk to the house. "No idea. It's all been a bit of a rush with you having to bail out of the States a bit early. We got the word that they've found Mulgrew, by the way. Reports are that the chambermaid found him after your plane had taken off. As far as we know they haven't made the connection with you two yet."

"We have somebody in the local police there?" Flaherty asked.

"Paddy, you know we have friends everywhere, or at least people who will sell us information. We'll be kept in touch, never fear."

"Anything new on the killings in New York or Boston?"

Eoin pushed open the door and went inside. "Come on in. No, nothing new on either killing. Not even sure they have connected them to each other or to you yet. Let's hope it stays that way. You don't want any difficulties when you go back to the US."

Billy put down his bag and guitar. "We're definitely going back then?"

Eoin opened the fridge door and took out three beers which he handed around. "VB, that's the good beer around here. It'll wet your whistle after that long flight. And yes, you'll be going back. You're lined up to talk to a bunch of people who would like to invest serious money in Ireland's future government. There might be a couple of those down here, but nowhere near as lucrative as the States, so you'll be back there for sure."

Flaherty put down his half-finished can of beer and yawned. "That's enough for me. I'm for me bed."

"Right then, let me show you your rooms and we'll talk more in the morning. If you wake up, don't wander outside. The dogs are OK once they know you, but not safe until then. I'll introduce you tomorrow."

Chapter 40

"Eoin, much as I enjoy the chance of a holiday, it's been three weeks now and all I've seen of Australia is your farm. Are we going to do anything anytime soon?"

Cleary finished his beer in one swallow and stood up. "I'll get us another beer while Flaherty finishes the cooking."

Billy leaned back and watched the sun just starting to dip behind the line of trees in front of the farmhouse. He nodded as the ice-cold can of beer was thrust into his hand a moment later.

"Now, son, we have to be patient. It's all part of the game. We stay out of sight until we get the word from Belfast that we can start the fundraising again. Until then, we sit out on this veranda, in the warm evening sun, and enjoy a cold beer and a yarn or two."

"Well, we've got the sun and the beer is certainly cold, but you've never been too forthcoming with the yarns. So now, why is it you're hiding here on this hobby farm? Are you one of the ones the British army wants to get their revenge on?"

Cleary sipped his beer and sighed in contentment. "I'm not convinced about this army revenge theory. The people we were up against in the old days are retired now and way past any need for revenge. At least, that's what I think, but if there were such a group they would want me for sure. I was the one who did the Hyde Park and Regent's Park jobs."

168

"They were bombings, were they?"

"That they were, right in the centre of London where the army thought they were safe. Made quite a fuss in the newspapers. It was pretty effective, even if I say so myself."

"So why would they particularly want you and not the other bombers?"

"Not just the army. Those two bombings had a negative effect in the US, so the IRA council were not best pleased about them, even though they authorised the two bombs. I think they told me to get the hell out of Ireland to deflect the negative comments from themselves. They put the word out among the nationalists that I had broken the rules and been punished. The suckers fell for it, but I ended up here. Trouble was, my wife wouldn't come here and leave her old ma behind, so she left me and I paid more of a price for the cause."

"Well, you can't just leave it there. What happened?"

Cleary stood up and looked down at Billy. "Tell you what, we'll go in for dinner now and afterwards I'll get out a bottle of the finest Bushmills Whiskey. I've been saving it for an occasion, but a night of tall tales about the old days might do just as well."

Billy picked up his empty beer cans and stood up. "Just as long as you tell the story, I'll help you with the Bushmills for sure."

Chapter 41
20th July 1982

Cleary settled himself on the veranda and picked up the glass of amber liquid. "You can never tell a good story without a glass of the Bushmills in hand."

"Well, I hope the story lives up to the whiskey, Eoin, and the meal, of course, Paddy."

"Right then, it was the summer of 1982 and I'd been part of an active service unit operating on the mainland for some time. The idea was to bring some trouble to the English as they didn't seem to mind about the Troubles in Ireland. We'd mounted a few bombings and got a lot of attention, but the boys back in Belfast passed the word that they wanted what they called 'a spectacular'."

"We started looking round for likely targets and we decided that for maximum publicity it had to be in central London. Somewhere the press could get to quickly and where there were plenty of tourists and office workers to see what we could do. We spent quite a while deciding, and once we'd spotted the targets the planning took a while as well. This had to work out if it was to be what the boys back home wanted."

Billy set his glass down on the rough table. "You said targets?"

"Targets, yes. We decided to hit in two places on the same day to get their heads spinning. The idea was that the police and ambulance people would be dealing with the first incident and we'd bang off another not far away.

"Anyway, if you'll let me go on, the first bomb I made was about twenty-five pounds of gelignite with around thirty pounds of nails packed around it. The nails were a favourite of mine as they acted like poor man's shrapnel and did a lot of damage. We mounted the bomb in an old blue Morris Marina car that we'd stolen the day before and we parked it up on the South Carriage Drive in Hyde Park."

"So what was the target in a park?

"Soldiers. We'd seen that the Household Cavalry rode past there every day from their barracks in Knightsbridge to Horse Guards Parade. It was all part of the Changing of the Guard ceremony that happens every day in summer. We wanted to get the foot guards, but there was nowhere to leave the car on their route. So we set the bomb and retired to a safe distance to watch the fun. The bomb was triggered by remote control, so we had to be there anyway to make sure we got the target.

"We waited and then we saw them coming along, a troop of cavalry in their blue jackets with shiny breastplates and helmets with their red plumes. They were mounted all on black horses. Beautiful animals to make an Irishman's heart soar. I had second thoughts there for a second or two when I saw those horses, but we were committed. They came alongside the car and I pressed the trigger button on the remote. There was a hell of a bang and the car blew to bits. The nails and bits of car body flew and slashed into the target. We could hear the screaming across the

171

park. I'd heard men scream before, so that didn't bother me, but I'd never heard a horse scream in pain and that wrenched my gut, I have to confess.

"We stood and watched as the smoke cleared and we could see we'd blown the troop apart. There were bodies across the road and there were wounded men and horses struggling to rise. The noise from the horses was terrible. The police started to arrive quickly, so we turned away and walked to the Knightsbridge underground station and we were away before the ambulances arrived.

"We changed trains a couple of times in case we were being followed and then we got off at the Baker Street station near Regent's Park. The second target was in the park, so we walked in to where we could see it. There were posters on the notice boards advertising a band concert by The Royal Green Jackets military band. They were going to play the tunes from 'Oliver!' that was popular at that time. I'd put the bomb under the bandstand the night before and we'd got it on a timer, so there was nothing on us if we'd been stopped.

"The band started playing and they were pretty good, so there were quite a few civilians around watching them. I'd made the bomb with no nails this time and angled it so it would blow upwards under the band. The idea was that the blast would miss the people around watching, but they would get to see everything and that should cause a panic. It worked out fairly well too.

"At about five minutes to one the bomb went off, just as we'd planned. The blast went up through the floor of the bandstand and ripped them up. There were a few injuries among the civilians, but none of them got killed, so that was a good thing. The IRA had wanted a spectacular and we gave it to them. There was a hell of a fuss in the press for days after."

Billy took a swig from his glass to clear the foul taste in his mouth. "So what were the casualties from all this?"

"Four of the cavalry died and there were seven horses that died or had to be put out of their misery. Seven of the bandsmen died and there were eight civilians injured. I think that was my best day's work for the cause."

"You're proud of that?"

"It was a war, Billy, make no mistake. Just because the British refused to call it a war didn't make it any less of one. Nasty things happen in wars."

Chapter 42

Flaherty stumbled on a loose rock as he climbed back up the river bank. He kept hold of his rod and the bag of fish he was carrying.

"Nearly lost our dinner there, Billy boy. Would have had to be burgers again."

Billy smiled. "We wouldn't want that now, would we? Any chance you can persuade Eoin to go into town and get something different? I'm getting pretty sick of the stuff he has in his freezer and we're running low on beer."

The older man chuckled. "And I guess you want to go with him?"

"I wouldn't mind, but I'm pretty sure he wouldn't wear that, until he gets clearance from Belfast. He seems very careful to do just as he's told, so he does."

Flaherty nodded and sighed. "With good reason. These AVNI killings have got the army council spooked. They are turning over every rock they can think of to find out who the hell is doing this to us."

"We're so far away, surely they can't know we are here?"

Flaherty stopped and turned around. "You don't understand, Billy. It's got worse. Three other volunteers from the old days have been killed in the States. People we've never been near. This AVNI thing is spreading and with the armed struggle ready to kick off again we need to put a stop to it right now."

"But to be honest, if these AVNI people are really old soldiers then surely they're going to be past it by now? They must be past retirement age, most of them. Are we sure it's not an IRA splinter group trying to take over? There's been plenty of them over the years. Or could it not be an offshoot of the UDA or another Unionist group?"

"And there you have the problem, Billy," Flaherty agreed. "It could be any number of groups and we need to make sure that you and me don't lead them to any of our serious backers. If that gets known to the authorities there could be hell to pay when we get back."

Billy sighed and hefted the strap of the fishing tackle box on his shoulder. "So bloody burgers and similar crap it is, unless we catch fish. At least that gives us a reason to get out of the house. I'm sick of looking at those walls, I have to tell you."

"Me, too, if I tell the truth, but we have to be patient, and this is a fine place for us to keep out of sight and that's a fact."

"Are you still not letting me contact Ma? She'll be getting worried that she hasn't heard from me all the time we've been away."

"Can't risk it, Billy. Phone calls and emails are too easy to track nowadays. That's why I'm so careful."

They walked on until they came in sight of the farmhouse with its equipment sheds and machinery garage behind it. They walked into the back door to the kitchen and Flaherty dropped the fish in the sink. Billy took the rods back out to the store shed and came back in to find the fish already being gutted, filleted and skinned.

"You need any help with that?"

"No thanks, Billy, but you could chop an onion and some peppers, then fry them up with a bit of chopped tomato for the sauce."

"Fair enough. I thought Eoin was supposed to be doing that while we were out?"

"He was, but the idle bastard doesn't seem to have done a hand's turn in here. Hasn't even washed the damned dishes from this morning."

"Maybe he's sleeping off that hangover he was due after the whiskey last night. He was packing away far more than his fair share for sure."

Flaherty chuckled. "Well, you go wake him up. He needs to suffer a little before I feed him my special fish recipe. He is a Catholic, after all; he knows about penance for sin."

Billy grinned and walked through into the living room. He had expected to find Cleary sprawled in his chair and snoring like a pig, as usual, but he wasn't there. He checked the bedroom and that was empty as well. He looked out of the front window to ensure that the rusty white pickup truck was still where it had been left. He went back into the kitchen.

"He's done some kind of vanishing act, or he's found somewhere new to sleep it off. He's not in the house."

"Has he gone to town for more supplies?"

"Can't have, the Ute is still there."

Flaherty slowly put down the filleting knife and wiped his hands on the towel next to him. He looked across the room at Billy and then walked around the table to the larder door. He stepped inside and reached up to the top shelf to push the cereal packets to one side. His hand came down gripping the heavy revolver that Cleary kept there as insurance.

"You don't think it's happened again?"

Flaherty checked that the gun was fully loaded and snapped it shut. "I don't know, but we need to find him right now. Get yourself a knife out of the drawer, then stay with me and watch my back."

"Who watches my back?"

"That'll be me. Now come on."

They went out through the front door and Flaherty scanned the soil outside the house for any new vehicle tracks. Then he nodded towards the first of the sheds. He stood back with the revolver at the ready while Billy pulled the door open. They went into the sun-dappled shadow where the light streamed through broken wall boards. Flaherty waved Billy forward with his gun and stood watching while he searched around the piled junk and rusty tools.

"Nothing. Could he have gone with someone else?"

"He could have done any damned thing while we were by the river. You remember that, Billy: you and me we were together all morning and never out of each other's sight."

"You do think it's happened again. What the hell am I supposed to do with a bloody kitchen knife if the killer's still here?"

"We don't know anything yet. Get your arse in gear and we'll check the other shed."

Together they walked across the dusty ground and went into the second shed. Again Billy searched while Flaherty covered him and again there was nothing unusual. Billy looked at the older man, who said nothing, but pointed to the machinery garage across the yard.

They were wary as they came to the larger storage building and Billy stopped short as he saw the body propped up against the wheel of a battered red tractor.

"Check his pulse."

"You think I really need to with that bloody great gash across his throat? If his heart was still beating there'd be blood gushing all over."

Billy squatted down next to Cleary and touched his shoulder. The bloodied mess that had been their drinking companion slowly slipped to one side and hit the filthy floor of the barn. As he rolled they could see the handle of the knife still protruding between his shoulder blades. The back of his shirt was torn with half a dozen gory stab wounds.

Billy looked up. "He's dead as mutton, Paddy. What the hell do we do now?"

Flaherty stared down at his old friend for a long moment before he shook himself out of it and glanced around him. "We clear our stuff up and make sure there's no sign we were ever here. Then we load our stuff into the Ute and get some distance between us and this place. We'll abandon the pickup somewhere in the city."

"What about Cleary? Do we bury him?"

"Billy boy, we were never here, so how can we bury him? We leave him to be found, that's what we do, and nobody any the wiser. Then I need to find a computer and report this back to the army council in Belfast. You make sure you remember we were together when this happened. There's going to be some difficult questions asked."

Billy packed his bag in a hurry and grabbed his guitar case. He put both in the back of the Ute and saw Flaherty coming out of the farmhouse with his own luggage.

"Ready?"

"Not yet." Flaherty heaved his bag into the bed of the pickup. "You go in Eoin's room. He keeps a nine millimetre automatic, with a silencer, in his bedside drawer. We might as well take it with us. I'll keep the revolver."

Billy was back in minutes. "It's not there. There's a space in the drawer where I guess it was, but there's no sign of it, and yes, I did look around. I did find a small .22 pistol, though."

"Shit! If the coppers find the 9mm when they come for the body they might add two and two. Nothing we can do about it now. Keep the .22 and get in, we're leaving."

"Where are we going?"

Flaherty started the engine and looked across the cab. "First into Sydney, where we drop this off

179

in a back street somewhere. Then we shack up in a hotel while I call another of our contacts. Most of all I need to find a computer, to report in."

Chapter 43

Sydney was quiet on that Sunday afternoon. They drove into the King's Cross area and found a quiet back road to park the Ute. Flaherty left the keys in the ignition in the hope that one of the layabouts they could see around them would steal it and move it somewhere else. They walked along to the main road and turned towards the centre of the city looking for a hotel.

"That looks like the place for us, Paddy."

"Which one?"

"Over there, the Ibis. Nothing too flashy, but not too far from everything."

Flaherty walked to the edge of the road and waited to cross. "We'll see if they've got rooms for us. We need to get off the street before we get noticed wandering around humping our baggage."

The rooms were clean and modern and Billy was surprised at how comfortable the bed was when he tried it. He went back down to the lobby to wait for Flaherty. Most of the people wandering in and out ignored him and those that looked at him didn't take much notice. He relaxed and waited.

Flaherty walked up behind him. "Right then, Billy, I've found out where there is an Internet café. I'm going to go down and send the messages I need to."

"If we need to keep reporting in, why not buy a laptop and use the Wi-Fi here?"

"Basic precautions, Billy Boy. The monitoring people at GCHQ can pick up our location if we send from here. If we send from different places on different machines they will know we're in Sydney, but not exactly where."

"You think the British are looking for your messages?"

Flaherty nodded. "I'm stone-cold certain of it. They know who the big players are back home and they will monitor their computer traffic. That's why I use a code so they know where the message comes from, but not what it's about."

"These are the people who broke the Enigma code during the Second World War and you think your code will beat them?"

Flaherty gave Billy a slow smile. "I do. See, we use a book code. I have a certain book and the guy the other end has the same book. I give him a set of numbers that indicate the page, line and word I have chosen. Nobody can break that unless they know the book and the exact edition."

"So what happens if someone blabs?"

"I've got a few books I can use, so I have. We rotate them to keep the British listeners guessing. I've memorised the order they come in, so there is nothing for anyone to find if we get stopped and searched, just some innocent-looking books."

"All good, but how do you tell them about Eoin without using his name?"

Flaherty chuckled. "Good question. We've all got a code name made up of numbers that look like the same code, but even if they had the book they would be meaningless."

"So what am I?"

"You? You're 47-21-05. Page 47, line 21, word 5. If they look that up they just get a random word that tells them nothing. Good, isn't it?"

Billy nodded. "So I'll go for a walk down to the harbour bridge while you do that. I can come back here to meet you for dinner."

"No, no, that's not happening. We stay together anytime we're out of here. You're my alibi and I'm yours when the finger-pointing starts. The boys back home are going to be looking for who the hell is identifying our people and we're going to be first in the frame again, for sure."

"So I get to sit in the Internet café and watch you send emails, do I?"

"That's about the size of it. It won't take long, I've got the message coded up already and then we can walk down the hill and see some of the sights. It'll be the morning before we need to find another computer to get the replies."

"Replies? So how many of these messages are you sending?"

"Just two. One to my handler in Belfast and one to our next contact in Australia. I'm not even sure where he is. Probably not Sydney."

Chapter 44

"Wake up, Billy, we're leaving."

"At this time of the morning? Give me a break." He put the phone receiver back down on the bedside rest and turned over. Seconds later it rang again. He swore quietly and picked it up.

"What?"

"Don't feck about, Billy, I'm serious. We're being picked up at the front of the hotel in half an hour. So get your arse out of bed and get packed."

"What about breakfast, for God's sake?"

"We'll get something at the airport. Now move!"

Billy put the phone down again and fought his way out from under the covers before stumbling to the bathroom. The shower and shave woke him up and he was downstairs in the lobby waiting for Flaherty in twenty-five minutes. The older man came out of the elevator and waved to Billy to follow him down the stairs to the front door.

"Shouldn't we check out?"

"Already done, and there's our taxi. Come on, don't hang about. We've just got time to get to the airport and get you fed before boarding. Unless you want to eat airline food again?"

Billy put his bag and guitar case in the taxi and straightened up. "You can keep that airline crap, so you can. I'll find something decent at the airport."

Flaherty grinned. "Good man yerself, now get in and we'll be gone."

The taxi dropped them off outside the departure doorway of the long, low, blue terminal building of Sydney International Airport. Billy waited while Flaherty paid and then followed him into the terminal. They checked their bags and headed for the security checks clutching the boarding cards for QANTAS Flight QF840 to Darwin.

Billy held his tongue until they were well clear of the security gate. "Why the hell are we going to Darwin? Are we back on the fundraising again?"

"OK, listen. We've got new instructions from the boys. We're to be the bait."

"Bait? What the hell does that mean?"

"We've got two good friends up in Darwin and they are going to watch our backs. One will be in the open and be bait like us. The other will keep his head down and watch for who comes sniffing round us. We're to stop these AVNI bastards now and Darwin is the place to do it."

"What's so special about Darwin then?"

"It's a relatively small city so a newcomer can be spotted. In truth, though, it's more about the people who will be helping us. Both of them are enforcers from the old days."

"Like Mulgrew, and much good it did him."

"Not like Mulgrew. He was a thug. I told you there was something wired up wrong in his head. These two are cold, calculating individuals, but clever with it. They've done some stuff, I can tell you."

"OK, so if we are bait, then why did you take the gun off me?"

Flaherty sighed. "Because you'd never get it on the aircraft. I packed them both up and sent them as parcel post. They'll be there not long after us and our friends can probably lend us something in the meantime."

Billy paused and looked around him. "First things first: I want some breakfast and some strong coffee before we get on the plane. How long is the flight?"

"According to the booking website, four hours and forty minutes. We should land about half past one this afternoon."

"Just in time for lunch." Billy smiled.

As they came out of the air-conditioned arrivals hall some five and a half hours later the sticky heat hit them. Billy could feel the sweat prickling on his skin within seconds and a trickle ran down his spine before they reached the car waiting at the kerb. The dark threatening clouds were rolling in from the north-east and the hot wind was pushing the dust along the street.

Flaherty opened the car door and Billy felt the cold of the air conditioning waft across his feet. The driver looked around and watched them as they climbed in.

"Welcome to Darwin and a nice cool day it is for you."

Billy wiped the sweat from his brow. "You've got to be kidding?"

The driver chuckled. "So I am. It gets like this just before one of our tropical storms and

186

we're about to get one any time now. I'm hoping to be back at the house before it breaks or the road becomes a bit of a problem."

Flaherty turned around in the front seat. "Billy, this is Sean, and Sean, this is Billy. Billy was just supposed to help with the fundraising, but it's turned a bit more serious now."

Sean nodded as he turned the car out onto the main road. "So I hear. We've been working up a plan to catch this bastard, if he tries anything here. Molly will run you through it after lunch."

"Molly? The other enforcer is a girl?"

"Molly is my wife and watch what you say to her. She gets short-tempered in this weather. She misses the soft Irish mornings around Carrickfergus."

"So why not go back there?"

"Let's get you home first. I'll tell you about us this evening, over a cold one. Then you can tell if you're in good hands or no."

Chapter 45

The threatening clouds built up, and despite the heat it got progressively darker until Sean had to turn the headlights on. They drove past a wire fence hung with no trespassing signs and swung into a gateway that opened at the touch of remote control button. Billy glanced out of the rear window to see the gate swing closed behind them. The car juddered over the rough hard-packed earth in front of the wide bungalow with the wraparound veranda.

The car stopped and they climbed stiffly out before retrieving their luggage and walking on to the veranda. Sean opened the screen door just as a massive peal of thunder ripped the sky and the deluge began. Billy turned and watched in wonder as the hard earth in front of the house was turned to a splattering pool of mud in seconds. The wire fence and the gate vanished behind a wall of teeming water and the temperature started to drop.

A soaking wet dog slunk around the corner and shook itself before nuzzling Sean's hand and then sniffing the visitors curiously. It wagged its tail once and went to lie down under the swing seat that hung with chains from the veranda roof.

"Let's get you inside. This will go on for a while," Sean shouted over the roaring noise of the rain on the roof.

It was no quieter inside and Sean gave up and just pointed at Billy and then to a door at the back of the room. Flaherty was directed to another. They dropped their bags in the rooms and returned to the open-plan living room where Sean was waiting with-ice cold tins of beer. The condensation was already running down them as they took one each.

"Where's Molly?" Flaherty called.

"She went to get in the food supplies we need for having you as guests. She'll probably wait until this eases off. It can be a hairy drive in a storm."

Conversation was difficult and patchy for another half hour and then the noise level started to drop as the worst of the storm moved on. Billy stood at the window and watched the rain ease and then the sea of mud started to dry out as the parched earth drank deeply. Another half hour passed before a shiny yellow Land Rover pulled in through the gate and he got his first sight of Molly.

He was startled that someone this beautiful could be an enforcer. From what he knew of the volunteers given that job, he had expected a harridan. Her long blonde hair was tied back in a long pony tail and her delicate features showed little sign of make-up. Even walking across the muddy ground there was an elegance about her and the tight shorts and man's shirt showed off her figure to advantage.

She pushed the door open with her foot and came in with the box of groceries in her arms. "Well, come on then, boys, help a girl unload the car, why don't ye? Flaherty, good to see you again. There's your package on the front seat. I checked the post office while I was in town."

Sean and Billy went to the back of the Land Rover while Flaherty went to the cab to collect his parcel. The cardboard boxes were soon unloaded and taken into the kitchen area where Molly was stacking the cupboards.

She looked over her shoulder. "So is someone going to tell me who this one is then?"

"Sorry, Molly," Flaherty said. "This is Billy. He's the singer who was helping me with the fund-raising before it all turned pear-shaped."

She looked him up and down. "So are you any good at the singing then, Billy? We could do with a tune or two tonight after dinner."

"I – I'll do what I can," Billy stuttered.

Molly smiled at him, knowing full well the effect she had on younger men.

"What's the matter, Billy? You look a bit stunned."

"Oh, oh no, just a bit tired from the early morning and the flight, I guess."

She winked at him. "Well, if that's all it is, that's fine. You'll feel better after lunch. It's just sandwiches since my idle husband didn't make anything while I was out. Is that all right with everyone?"

Billy knew it wasn't a question, so he kept his mouth shut and the other two men just nodded. He watched her surreptitiously as she moved around the kitchen slicing bread and putting the food together. He couldn't for the life of him work out how old she was. If she had been part of the armed struggle then she must be older than she looked. He was surprised that the things she must have done had not left their mark on her.

He sat quietly through lunch while the others chatted about the old days and reminisced about mutual acquaintances. Their hosts went quiet when Flaherty told them about the deaths that had followed them across the US and now into Australia. Molly picked up the empty plates and took them into the kitchen before returning and sitting back down at the table.

"We've got a plan. Sean here is going to be with you as bait. Nobody knows my past and the only reason I'm here is because I'm married to that one. When he had to get out of Ireland I came with him. We let it be known that we met in Melbourne when he first came over, so if your stalker asks around I'm not going to be a target. That gives us the home field advantage."

Flaherty nodded and leaned forward with his elbows on the table. "Well, I'd never believe you were old enough to have done some of the things I know you have, so I guess anybody looking for us would think the same. How do we go forward from here then?"

"The three of you stay together around the house. You'll be seen and identified, that's all to the good, but because you are together he can't hit you easily. We think that means he or they will hit at night and try and take you out one at a time. It means they can sneak up on the house and do it through a window or sneak in and make their play."

"How do we stop that?"

Molly smiled. "We don't, I do. I'm going to work nights while you are here. I'll sleep in the day and at night I'll be outside or in the window seat, with the night vision goggles on, waiting for anyone coming on to the property."

"What happens if nobody comes?"

"Then we know they have lost track of you and you're in the clear. Once we know that, you can get back to your fundraising in the States."

"Not here?"

Molly shook her head and Billy watched her golden hair swing around her face. "No, the boys have decided that the big money is in the US. You're not going to pick up enough down here so you'll be off back there once we have this monkey off your back."

"All sounds good," Flaherty said. "What about getting rid of the body?"

Sean grinned at Molly. "Did you not see all that open rugged country as you flew in? We take a body out there and leave it for the dingoes. It'll just be scattered, bleached bones in a week. Nobody goes off the beaten path up here, so nobody is going to find it."

"Not even the Aborigines?"

Sean shook his head. "Even if they were to find it they'd just walk on by. They don't need any more trouble from the police. Anyhow, there's no reason to think they'd be out where I've got planned."

Flaherty nodded slowly. "From your mouth to God's ears."

Chapter 46

He woke sweating in the middle of the night. There was no air conditioning in this bedroom and, even with the windows flung wide, it was way too hot to sleep. He climbed off the damp sheet and walked across to stand by the window. There was not a breath of air and the moonlight showed him another massive bank of clouds moving in for another storm. He gave up and wandered through into the living area to get a glass of water.

He was stood by the sink when he heard her soft voice from behind him. "Can't sleep then, Billy?"

He turned and looked around, but could see nobody in the darkened room. "No, I'm not used to the heat. I don't know how you manage."

"You get used to it after a while and we have the aircon in the rooms we use most often. Sorry about putting you in that room, but it's all we've got, unless you want to bunk with Flaherty?"

Billy chuckled. "Have you heard him snore? I'll get more sleep on my own even with the heat."

He could see her now in the gloom, sitting in the armchair that had the view out of two windows at the corner of the room. She lifted the night vision goggles off her eyes and pointed to the chair opposite.

"You can come and keep me company if you like. It's pretty boring watching the rats and the dingoes wander by."

He put the glass down on the side table and sat. "Looks like there's another of those storms coming."

"Not surprised, it's the season for them. Anyway, they drop the temperature quite a bit, at least for a while. You should be able to get some sleep then."

"If I can ignore the roar of water, pounding the roof."

"Ah yes, there is that. In the early days, I had to take sleeping tablets every other night to get some sleep or I'd have lost it and slaughtered someone. Then we got the aircon and now it's fine."

Billy sipped his water and gazed at her. The thin moonlight outlined her small nose and high cheekbones.

"You talk about killing so casually."

"Ah now, Billy, appearances can be deceptive. I know what you see when you look at me and that was the same thing the soldiers saw, when they stopped me at roadblocks. It made me useful to the cause and that's why they recruited me."

"So what did they have you doing?"

As the rain stared to pound the roof she took off the goggles and laid them beside her. "Pretty certain nobody is going to be sneaking about in this lot. So what did they have me do? Let's see, there was moving weapons around, then chatting to the soldiers to find out what they were intending to do, things like that."

"Paddy said you and Sean were enforcers."

He saw her blonde hair catch the dim light as she nodded. "That came later. Sometimes people have to be kept in line. Not just the volunteers. Sometimes we had to send a message to the civilians to make sure they did as they were told. Then sometimes we'd hear about people helping the army or the police and that had to be dealt with. Once in a while we'd provide security when the bombs were being placed to make sure nobody interfered with that."

"Sounds like you were pretty heavily involved in it all?"

"That's true, we both were. Trouble was, the police identified Sean, so we had to get out before the British hit squad found him and, like the dutiful wife, I had to come along as well. If they'd known some of the strokes I pulled they'd have been after me, too, for sure."

"What kind of strokes?" Billy asked.

Chapter 47
10th March 1971

"It was my first job for the boys. I was still at school when they told me I was needed. Hell, I was nervous, but they didn't tell me what the outcome would be. If they had I might not have done it. I met Sean during this so then I was hooked. He was so handsome back in those days."

"I'm sure he was, but what was the task they gave you?"

"They knew that soldiers used to go into the city centre pubs in Belfast during their off-duty time. They thought they were fairly safe there as not many soldiers had been killed by then and then only during riots. So I was sent into the pub to get picked up and when I had a fish on the hook to tell them I was going to a party and to invite them along."

"How did you know which ones were soldiers? Presumably they weren't in uniform?"

"Ah, they stood out like sore thumbs, so they did. Short haircuts, clean clothes and accents that weren't from Ireland. So anyway, I saw three of them at the bar and I went up and stood nearby. They started chatting to me straight away. They had Scottish accents, so I could tell they were from the garrison just up the road. They were dead keen on me, I could tell, and we carried on talking while they tried to impress me the way young lads do. After a while I told them I had to go, as I was on my way to a party at my friend Morag's house. They tried to persuade me to stay with them instead, so that's when I asked them if they wanted to come with me. They'd had a couple of beers so they weren't thinking sensibly and they all thought I was going to make all their birthdays come at once, so they agreed.

"There was a car waiting outside and I introduced them to the girl who was driving. She was a bit older than me, maybe nineteen, and she was pretty as well. From then on there was no question that they would come with us. They all piled in the car and we set off with them laughing and chatting to both of us girls. Once we got out into the country one of them said he needed to relieve himself, as we knew they would after all the beer. The driver, I forget her name, said she would stop when we got to a place where it was safe. She said she didn't want to lose her licence by stopping somewhere else."

"And I take it that it wasn't safe at all?" Billy asked.

"That's right. She drove on for a couple of more miles and then pulled over so the three lads could get out and relieve themselves. They were standing in a line at the side of the road, peeing into the ditch, when Sean appeared from nowhere. He walked up behind them silently and they never saw him coming. He had a pistol in his hand with a silencer on it. I couldn't believe it when he raised it up and shot the first lad in the back of the head. He swung left and did the same to the next lad. The third one turned round and Sean shot him in the chest. They all tumbled into the ditch and we left them there after Sean had checked they were dead."

"How did you feel about that?"

"I was shocked to start with, but then I was excited. More excited than I had ever been and I wanted more of it. That was the first time I had sex as well, with Sean in the back of the car. The sex was good, but the killings had excited me more and I think he knew it. After that they used to call me out for other jobs and eventually I was given a gun and I was allowed to do my own killings."

"And you enjoyed them as well, I guess?"

"The first one was amazing. I was so excited I almost wet myself while I was waiting. Then afterwards I was sick as a dog, but it had been an amazing feeling and it got better every time. I was never sick again."

"No wonder Sean warned me to be careful what I say to you."

"A wise man, my Sean is. He knows I get short-tempered this time of year and somehow the storms make me want to go back to the old days and feel that rush again. But we're under orders to stay off the radar down here and to wait until we are called back to Ireland as the armed struggle starts again."

"Do you know how they'll use you?"

"There's talk of us taking out a couple of Muslims in England so that they take to the streets and tie up the security services before we step up to the plate in Ireland. We'll see how that turns out. Now don't you think you'd be better getting some sleep?"

Chapter 48

Breakfast was a quiet meal with Molly tired out from her night's watch. Once finished, Billy volunteered to do the dishes while Flaherty checked around the house with Sean. Molly went to get some sleep, ready for her next night of watching and waiting.

With the plates and cups put away he went outside and sat on the shady veranda. The two men came around the corner of the house and sat down with him in the wooden garden chairs.

"Anything?"

"No, Billy. We checked around all the fences, but saw no footprints or any other sign that we were being watched."

"I can't imagine there would be footprints after that storm last night. I wouldn't let a dog out in that, so our AVNI friend and his mates will have stayed in the dry."

Sean nodded. "Probably right. Anyway the dog should be able to come back from the vet today, or at least I hope so. Damn fool cut his foot on a broken bottle, so he's been in getting it treated. Big soft lump he is, but he barks when anybody he doesn't know is about."

Flaherty smiled. "So does that mean we can expect Molly's company during the day?"

Sean sighed and stood up. "No, that's not her plan. If this bugger turns up she wants to top him and that's likely to be at night. Anyway, I'm making some tea. You both want some?"

The day dragged on and Billy tired of watching the small dust devils spinning across the barren yard in front of the house. He went into his sultry room and retrieved his guitar before taking himself around the back of the house away from Molly's bedroom window so as not to disturb her. He tuned the old instrument and wiped the dust off it before he started to play quietly to himself. He played the soft Irish tunes he loved and avoided the rebel songs that had brought him here. He sighed and hoped he could play the fine music of Ireland when this journey was over.

He played for hours, letting his mind drift and take him to the misted hills he loved. Then they took him to the streets of Belfast that he did not love. He recalled dimly the days of his childhood, when there had been soldiers on the streets in their camouflage uniforms and helmets. He didn't want to see that again in his home town. He didn't want to see the fear in his people's eyes.

He stopped playing and put the guitar down beside his chair. "That was nice, Billy. You play well."

He looked up and there was Sean leaning against the corner of the building with a smile on his face. "How about you play some more of that after dinner? Molly would love it. She longs to be back home and away from the heat and sweat we have here."

"So why don't you go home then? Ireland has calmed down after the troubles and the army isn't on the streets anymore."

Sean shook his head slowly. "Ah, Billy boy, there's people have long memories for certain things. The British had death squads, or at least I think they did. Probably their SAS men. They'd still like to have a quiet word with me about some things and I don't think I'd enjoy that too much, so I don't."

"What makes you think they had death squads?"

Sean sat down in the other chair that stood there and leaned back against the wall of the house. "Did you never hear of the killings in Gibraltar?"

"Gibraltar? Never heard about that."

"That was a success for the army, that's for sure. We sent an active service unit to Gibraltar to set a bomb off during the changing of the guard ceremony. They flew into Spain and hired two cars. They left the one with the explosives in it in Spain and drove over into the colony. They parked the car in the car park where the guard ceremony people assembled. The idea was to keep the parking space while they carried out surveillance before the bombing. Once they were ready they would bring the bomb over and switch the cars so the bomb car would be in the best place.

"Anyway, what they and we didn't know was that they had been spotted and an SAS unit was watching them. They were walking back towards the border to get the bomb car when they were challenged by the SAS troopers. The SAS claimed they made movements as if they were going for concealed weapons and they opened fire.

Turns out they didn't have any guns on them, but they were just as dead.

"Of course all our tame politicians and the left-wing media on the mainland made a fuss and called the SAS 'government assassins'."

Billy glanced at Sean. "Sounds like the SAS were justified in shooting these people, don't you think?"

"Truthfully, and just between us, yes, but what it did show us was that there were death squads hunting us, or at least that's the lesson we took from it. The bodies were flown back to Ireland and the funerals got a bit messy, that's for sure."

"Messy? What does that mean?"

"Tell you what. You give Molly a couple of songs this evening after dinner and I'll tell you the story. Deal?"

"Deal"

***

Flaherty cleared away the plates and put them into the sink to soak. Billy took out his guitar and settled in the corner of the room where he could feel the cool breeze from the air conditioning unit. Molly and Sean sat together on the sofa that looked like it had seen better days.

"What would you like to hear, Molly?"

"Something quiet to carry me away from here."

"Is it that bad here really?" Billy asked.

"No, it's not, but it isn't home and never will be."

Billy nodded and strummed his fingers gently across the strings. He played quietly and sang sweetly and the words of 'The Parting Glass' filled the room. Even the dog settled down and seemed to be listening. As he finished he looked up and saw the tear toll down Molly's cheek. She dashed it away and smiled at him.

"Will you play another?"

He played 'The Fields of Athenry' and saw that she was struggling to hold her emotions in check. He finished and she gave him a sad smile before she went to get a shower, before her night of watching.

Sean watched her go. "That was good, Billy, thanks. Now I think I promised you a story."

Chapter 49
19th March 1988

Sean filled the whiskey glasses and sat back into the sofa with a sigh. "Like I told, you the funerals got messy. The bodies of the ASU from Gibraltar were flown back and there was going to be a true Republican funeral. The organisers did a deal with the army, so that they would stay back and we would not have any uniforms or shots over the grave. Both sides kept to the agreement, but some UDA nutcase attacked the funeral, He was throwing grenades and shooting his pistol. He killed three people and wounded more than sixty. One of the photos from that day was of Gerry Adams of Sinn Fein sheltering behind a child. That gave the British a great laugh.

"One of the men killed was an IRA volunteer and we held his funeral on the 19th March. People were pretty incensed by the attack in the graveyard, so there was a big turnout and feelings were running high. The army understood that and they stayed back so as not to provoke any clashes. They'd even issued orders for all their people to stay out of the area.

"So anyway we were on the way to the Milltown Cemetery along the Andersonstown Road, with some black taxis leading us with the chief mourners when this car appears. One of the stewards waved at it to get it to turn out of the way, but it kept on coming straight at the front of the funeral. We all thought it was another Loyalist attack like we'd just had. Anyhow, it turned into a side road, mounting the pavement as it did so. There were mourners diving everywhere to get out of the way. The side road was blocked, so all of a sudden the car started to reverse rapidly back into the funeral procession. They then tried to drive out of the funeral, but there was a black taxi in the way."

"By now the crowd was well and truly wound up and they surrounded the car, beating on the roof and smashing the windscreen. Well, now, the driver pulled out an automatic pistol and fired a shot in the air to scatter the crowd. Then there was a dull roar and they surged back, attacking the car with a wheel brace and anything else they could lay their hands on, including a step ladder they grabbed from a press photographer. The two men in the car were dragged out and the crowd started to beat the hell out of them. They were searched and military ID cards were found so we knew they were soldiers. Then the beating got worse. They were stripped, kicked and pounded. A priest tried to stop it, but the crowd were having none of it.

"After more of this they were bundled into a taxi and taken just down the road to some waste ground near Penny Lane. People in the crowd knew who we were, so they called me and Molly over to do them. I put six shots into one of them and Molly put five into the other. Then we got the hell out of there as there was an army helicopter circling overhead. The priest came across as we were leaving and gave them the last rites.

"We put out a statement about an attack by the SAS being foiled by the IRA. It turns out they were actually from the Royal Signals and had nothing to do with the SAS."

Billy sat very still, looking at Sean. "Sounds pretty bloody awful."

"I suppose it was, and for sure the army would like to get hold of me for that one, I think."

Chapter 50

The heat still kept him from sleep, but he did not want to go into the living room and sit with Molly. He was struggling to believe that this lovely woman was a cold-blooded killer, yet it seemed to be true. Worse, she seemed to be excited by killing. Billy tried to suppress the feeling of revulsion and turned the pillow over to try and find some coolness to let him sleep.

He woke, bleary-eyed, in the morning with a pain behind his eyes from the restless night and the whiskey the evening before. He dressed and went in search of breakfast and coffee. The others were already at the table as he came in.

"You look like shit, Billy. Bad night?" Flaherty asked.

"Yes, thank you. That room needs aircon for sure."

Sean grinned. "We don't usually use it for guests. In fact, we don't usually have guests. That's our store room most of the time, so aircon isn't needed."

"I think I might try sleeping outside tonight. It has to be cooler than that oven."

Sean and Molly looked at each other and chuckled. "Billy lad, those bug screens on the window aren't for decoration. If you sleep outside the insects will eat you alive and we've got some big buggers round here."

Molly took pity on him. "I'll make you up a bed in here. I have the aircon running while I'm sitting up and you can share it."

"There's bacon by the cooker and some eggs in the fridge if you want to make yourself a fry-up. The coffee is fresh, too, so help yourself."

Billy nodded to Sean and instantly regretted it as the pain stabbed through his head. He poured the coffee into a cracked mug and drank half of it before he attempted to fry the bacon and eggs. Once he had that inside him he started to feel more human and even enjoyed the second coffee.

"So is there anything to do today? I thought I might take a walk round the area, see if there's any interesting wildlife or whatever."

"Tell you what, Billy," Sean said, "I'm going into town to get some more food and beer. You're welcome to come along and help if you want."

"That'll do. Better than sitting round here all day."

"About half an hour then and we'll be off. Anybody want anything special?"

They drove into Darwin and Billy looked around as they went. He could see the ocean sparkling between the buildings, but what struck him most was the amount of greenery. Parks were planted with wide-open swathes of grass and trees, but there was none of the lush green of Ireland. Here the green seemed to have been washed out of the plants by the sun and they had a pale dusty look to them. They passed a tennis club with masses of courts, all empty. Nobody, it seemed, wanted to play in the fetid heat.

The fierce air conditioning blast as they walked inside the supermarket hit Billy as though it was something physical and he felt his nostrils close with the shock of it. The shelves were well-stocked and he pushed the trolley around as Sean worked through his list.

Flaherty was waiting to help them unload as they returned to the house. Billy walked past the dog with his box of groceries and it didn't even raise its head. Some guard dog that one, he thought. With the Land Rover unloaded, he went into the bathroom and took a shower to get the sweat and dust off his skin before coming back out and flopping into a chair in front of the aircon unit.

"Paddy, how long are we staying here? This heat is getting to me."

"Good timing, Billy. I've had an email while youse were out. The boys think that these AVNI bastards have lost track of us so we can get back to the States and start up the fundraising again."

"I was hoping we were going home. Me ma will be getting worried, so she will. You haven't let me contact her for bloody weeks now."

"They want us in Chicago. There's a businessman there who we think can be persuaded to part with a wedge of cash for future favours, when Ireland is in our hands."

"Chicago? How the hell do we get there from here?"

"We fly, Billy boy. From here to Sydney, then we catch a flight to Houston Texas and from there we fly on to Chicago O'Hare. Should take just short of thirty hours."

"Christ, Paddy, thirty hours in cattle class seats. I'm going to be crippled."

"Not so. Economy from here to Sydney, but I've booked us in business class from there on. I think we deserve it after being stuck here in this sweatbox."

"That'll do me. When do we go?"

"Day after tomorrow. Damned early start, though. We'll have to be at the airport just before midnight."

"No problem."

"Start working out what you're going to be singing. There's plenty of Irish bars for our cover story, but this could be the big score for us."

"I thought the guy in Seattle was a big score?"

"He was, but this could be enough to let the struggle start up again, if we can convince him to fund us the way we hope."

Chapter 51

Molly and Sean drove them out to the airport and walked with them to the security area. She kissed Billy's cheek and whispered to him.

"Do your best to get the money, Billy. I want to go home. I want to see my sisters and my ma before it's too late.

He smiled at her. "I'll do my best to get you what you need."

She smiled back at him and then turned away with Sean and walked back towards the exit from the airport building. Billy watched them go and then walked through into the security check area with Flaherty.

"I wish I could take my guitar in the cabin with us. I'm always worried when it's in the hold."

"Never fuss. They haven't damaged it yet and it's in a good strong case. Besides, I'm not paying for an extra seat just so you can sit with it. It's cheaper to buy a new one if there's a problem."

"I'd prefer to keep the old one that I got off Seamus."

"Aye, your da would be proud to think you were using his old guitar to help the cause. Such a shame they got him that way, though. A man like him dead in a back alley is a tragedy for us."

Billy said nothing as he took off his shoes and put them on the inspection belt. He watched as they ran through the X-ray machine and then followed them through the arch of the metal detector. With his shoes back on they walked into the almost deserted departure hall and found a couple of chairs, to wait until their flight was called.

***

Sean waited in the Land Rover as Molly pulled the gate open when the remote control failed. She stood back as he drove in and pulled up in front of the house. He looked around as he got out.

"Where's the dog got to?"

"Oh, he'll be sleeping somewhere cool. You know he's a lazy old mutt."

"True enough. D'ye want anything before bed?"

"Not for me. It's been a long day."

She stopped as she turned the door handle. "Did you not lock this as we went out?"

"Of course I did. You know I always do."

"Well, it's not fecking locked now."

Sean turned back to the car and grabbed the heavy pistol from between the seats. Molly stepped to one side to let him enter first. He cocked the automatic and went in with it raised and ready. As he flipped on the light he heard the shot from behind him.

Molly had been silhouetted against the light of the open doorway and made a perfect target. The rifle bullet had taken her directly between the shoulder blades and ripped into her heart as it passed through and exited through her chest. She was flung forward into the doorpost, already dead before she hit the floor.

In his anger and grief, Sean forgot everything he knew and ran out through the door to take revenge without turning off the light. He jumped over Molly's body and paused for a second to look for the assailant. He had a split second to register the muzzle flash before the second heavy round slammed into his chest and threw him backwards into the house with his blood spewing onto the wooden floor. He lay staring up at the ceiling with the pistol still clenched in his hand.

He saw the man come through the door and look down at him with fierce blue eyes. "Well now, I wasn't expecting to be able to talk to either of you two. I must be losing my touch."

Sean struggled for breath. "Why? In the name of God, why?"

"Why? Because you and your pack of murdering bastards deserve it, that's why. It may have been a long time coming, but we don't forget a debt."

The stranger lifted the rifle until the barrel pointed at the wounded man's face and then he fired again, twice. He turned and looked down at Molly's body before he put two rounds into the back of her head as well. He dropped two calling cards on the bodies and then walked out without a backward glance, leaving the door open behind him. He swung the gate wide and wedged that open before walking along the side of the road to the car, which was parked behind a couple of scrubby bushes.

Behind the car was a filthy pond with slimy green weed across its surface. He wiped the rifle with an oily rag and then tossed it into the centre of the pool. The water would destroy any fingerprints long before the weapon was found, and connected to the theft from the back of the pub on the other side of Darwin.

Chapter 52

Billy dropped his bag by the side of the plastic chair and looked up at the annunciator board. The last leg of the journey from Houston to Chicago would take off in around ninety minutes. He was glad this was nearly over. The sleeping tablets had helped, but he was still sick to the back teeth of aeroplanes and airline food. Flaherty came back from the bar carrying two paper cups of coffee and sat down with a sigh.

"Nearly there then, Billy. Last leg and then we can get some proper sleep."

"Where are we staying this time? Not some shack in the country again, please."

Flaherty grinned and sipped his coffee. "Not this time. We're back in a decent hotel close to the airport. Our contact has arranged for the potential backer to come and meet us there."

"I take it they reckon we are in the clear then?"

"Sure as eggs is eggs. That rapid side trip out to Darwin will have lost any tail we might have had and it gave you a chance to meet the lovely Molly, didn't it?"

Billy put the almost tasteless coffee down. "I still can't believe she's a killer. She seemed so normal, but she told me that killing was exciting."

"What did you expect? A successful enforcer is not going to stay that way if they look like some kind of monster. That pretty face and that figure got her past many an army checkpoint back in the day. Young lads in uniform, starved of female company, were always distracted and, like you, they couldn't imagine she was the enemy."

"She told me how homesick she is. She wants to get away from that heat and back to the misty morning around Ballycastle, with the breeze coming in off the sea and Rathin Island just off the coast. On a clear day, she says you can see Scotland in the distance."

"You can see why. That muggy heat was getting me down and we were only there for days. They've been exiled down there for years."

"Why don't they move down to Sydney or Melbourne then?"

"They have their instructions, like the rest of us. They stay there to keep out of sight. The boys don't want groups of our wild geese flocking together and getting noticed. Anyhow, they'll be heading north again soon enough, if this works out when we meet our backer."

"She'll like that."

"Sure enough, and she'll like it better when the island of Ireland is united and under our control. Those two will be feted as heroes, as will many more of the people we bring home. And just think, Billy, you are a key part of this. The boys won't forget that, you know."

Billy smiled. "It would be good to be remembered for what we've done these last few weeks. Anyhow, that's our flight just popped up on the board. We'd better get down to the gate and hope the coffee on board is better than this dishwater."

Chapter 53

He could feel the grit of tiredness behind his eyes as he collected his guitar case and carried it out into the arrivals hall. Thirty hours travelling, cooped up in aircraft, was no joke, even if business class had been far more bearable. He felt dirty and sticky and in desperate need of a shower. He checked the guitar case for damage and was pleased to see that nothing untoward had happened to it in the various baggage holds.

"So where are we staying, Paddy?"

"Right by the airport. I've booked us into the Hilton Garden Inn. They had a deal on, so the price is a cracker for a place of that standard. We just need to find their airport shuttle and we can chill out. They've even got an indoor pool for you."

"Sounds good. So when is the first gig?"

"Not sure we even need a gig here unless we need a cover story. Maybe we can have you sing in the bar when our guest comes to visit. We'll see how it works out."

The shuttle had them at the hotel in minutes and the check-in was painless. Billy flung his bags on the bed before stripping and climbing into the shower. He soaked for a long time as the warm jets pounded him and made him feel human again. Dressed in clean clothes, he went down to the bar to find Flaherty already sitting on a stool with a tall glass on the bar. As he sat down the barman looked over at him with one eyebrow raised and he pointed at the beer in front of Flaherty.

"So then, are you wanting to tell me the plan?"

Flaherty waited until Billy's beer arrived and then nodded to one of the booths. They went and settled where they could not be overheard before he spoke.

"Now then, our contact round here has sounded out a businessman and he's interested. Now it's up to me to make a deal that will get us a big fat cash injection. He's coming in this evening to meet us here. If anybody was to ask, it's about signing you to his record label."

"He has a record label?"

"He has his fingers in many pies. Hotels, department stores, manufacturing, shipping, entertainment and yes, he has a record label. This guy is a serious player and the kind of money we need to get the armed struggle off the ground, and for us to take over the government of the whole damned island, is small change to this one."

"And he's on board with us?"

"So far, yes."

"Another of these Irish descendants, I guess?"

"Not this time. I'm pretty sure he's Greek. It seems he wants a base in Europe where his empire can expand and reach new markets easily. At least, that's the word I've been given. We'll see for sure when we talk to him."

"So what do you want from me?"

"Bring your guitar down to the bar tonight and, if anybody is taking too much interest, we'll have you give him a couple of songs so he can say

221

it's an audition. Like I told you, you're our cover story, just like always."

Billy finished his beer and stood up. "In which case I've got time to get some decent sleep before he gets here."

"You don't want to eat?"

"I do, but I want sleep more. I'll have dinner later, when our man gets here."

***

Four hours later, Billy walked back into the bar carrying his guitar in its case. Flaherty was sitting in the same booth speaking with a balding overweight man who looked up as he saw the guitar.

"So you're the one Paddy calls the Minstrel Boy?"

Billy held out his hand. "That's me, the wandering minstrel for the cause."

"Yanis Christophides. Sit then. We've only just met up and the waiter should be over anytime now."

The fat man turned his attention back to Flaherty. "Right then, I've heard the bullshit, so what's the offer?"

Flaherty smiled broadly. "Pretty much anything you want. We're ready to move soon. We've been undermining the Irish government and the British have taken their eye off the ball. We are going to get the Muslims to kick off with rioting in the streets, so that the security forces are tied up before we act. Our people are already in senior positions in the police in the North and in the judiciary. This is an apple that is ready to fall as soon as we pull at it."

The fat man rested his chins on his hand. "Assuming I fund this adventure, what's the offer for me?"

"Tell me what you need, and if we can do it, you can have it."

"That's pretty wide open. Are you sure you have that authority?"

"Listen, I've been in the IRA for years. I've done things that would make your toes curl. I'm trusted by the army council and I have the authority from them to make any deal that will get us to the restart of the armed struggle. It's going to be short and sharp this time because we are going to have done the full build-up before we act. So now, what would persuade you to back us?"

"Make a list. I want to be able to take over industrial sites without any interference from government. When I move my businesses in there will be no taxes and no bloody labour laws. You people guarantee to let me run my business without interference. If anybody tries to start a union I expect you people to stamp it out for me. I get to bring in anybody I want to work for me. The new government of Ireland defends me in the European Union and tells them to go to hell, if they try to interfere. How's that for starters?"

Flaherty considered and then nodded slowly. "Well, I don't see any major stumbling blocks. Of course there will need to be some personal contributions to certain people in the organisation.

Just a one time up-front payment should deal with that."

"Bribes."

"Let's say gratuities for services to be rendered."

"So you want me to pay these gratuities before I get anything from them?"

"You have to understand, this is going to be short, but violent. We will be risking our lives and the lives of the volunteers. Paying up front gets you some skin in the game and then we know you won't be pulling out and leaving us sucking our thumbs."

"I get that. All right, that matches up with what the other guy told me, so when do we do this?"

"As soon as you are ready. I have the bank account numbers for the relevant people here in the US. You put the funds in there to start with and then the funding of the uprising itself gets moved to our account in Holland. Then we get the weapons moved and we start."

The fat man's jowls rippled as he nodded. "And how long before you start after I make the payment? Then how long before the British cave in and give Ireland to the Irish?"

"From the payment arriving we can have the weapons bought and shipped to our people in a month. Their training is already in hand in the deserts of Libya where we still have friends. Once the struggle starts we think it should be between six months and a year before we succeed."

"That's pretty quick to take over a country," Christophides said with one eyebrow raised.

"We've been laying the groundwork for twenty years. We are playing the long game here and it's going to bear fruit, with your help."

The fat man sat back on the bench seat of the booth. "All right, I'm interested. What about this one, what does he get?"

Flaherty looked at Billy and smiled. "Billy? Well now, he has dreams of being a professional singer. What do you think about signing him to a recording contract? Should cost you very little and he could even make you some of your money back."

Christophides pointed at the guitar case. "Can you play that thing or is it just for show?"

"I can play it well enough."

"Fine then, give me a song and I'll see if you're worth my while."

While Billy was opening the case and taking out the guitar the Greek turned his attention back to Flaherty. "When he has finished I have a question for you. I want you to prove to me that you were active in the struggle and not just one of these big mouths I hear from now and then. Start thinking about an example for me."

Billy played three songs and sang along to them. The other bar patrons applauded and asked for more while Christophides just smiled.

"You've got the job, kid. I'll have the contract sent to you as soon as I get back to the office. Now then, Paddy, tell me a story."

Chapter 54
24th October 1990

Flaherty cleared his throat and took a swallow from his beer glass. "It was October, so the nights were long when we made our move. We were going to hit the border checkpoint at Coshquin, on the Buncrana Road. Trouble was, we had looked at it before and it was difficult to get near enough. What we wanted was to bomb it, but we didn't go in for suicide bombings like these Arab nutcases."

"So what did you do?"

"We worked out a new tactic that the army hadn't seen before so they wouldn't be ready for it. We called it a proxy bomb."

"How did that work?"

"Let a man tell his story and you'll find out. So we identified a man who was working at the army base as a cook. He was a Catholic and he'd been warned to stop it a couple of times, but he'd ignored the warnings. Some nonsense about showing an example to his kids, instead of sitting on his arse drawing unemployment benefits. Anyway, we couldn't let that defiance pass, so he was selected.

"We went to his house late at night and when he opened the door we forced our way in. We got his family down in the living room and made it very clear that if he didn't do as he was told they were going to die. Being a good family man there was not much he could do at that point. We took him in his own car across the border into County Donegal and put him into a van we had prepared there. He was chained into the driver's seat and told to drive to the checkpoint. He argued, but we put a photo of his family that we'd taken from his house in front of him as motivation and he went quiet.

"He drove off towards the border with one of our cars following him. As we got close to the checkpoint we armed the bomb remotely and then dropped back. We had one of our people observing to see what happened. She said she heard shouting and yelling as he got closer, but the soldiers couldn't understand him. He opened the door so they could hear him better. What he didn't know was that there was a second trigger to the bomb wired to the inside courtesy light. When the door opened power went to that and the bomb blew. It killed five soldiers and made a hell of a mess of the base. The operations room was destroyed and a number of vehicles badly damaged. We'd have killed more of the bastards, but they'd just built a mortar-proof bunker for the troops and they were off duty in there.

"We were well pleased with the results, so we used the same tactic again a few times. We made sure to pick people who were getting out of line so it sent a message to the civilians as well. It made the army jumpy, too, so we hoped they'd shoot someone by mistake so we could make a song and dance about army brutality, but that didn't work out."

Christophides was still for a moment, gazing at Flaherty. "That's damned cold. What happened to the family?"

"Of course it's cold, and that's why we are going to win this time. With us in the driving seat you can make vast profits in Ireland, never fear. And the family? We let them go so they could spread the word as a warning to others to obey the IRA."

Chapter 55

"Well then, Billy, how'd you like them apples? A recording contract for you and enough money for the boys, so that the cause can finally succeed. We've done it, boy! We're going home as heroes. Plus, the gratuities for me and the boys won't hurt at all. Should get us a fine welcome home."

"So are we going home now?"

"I'm going to email back to the council and get their confirmation that we can. As soon as we have that I'll book us the flights back to Belfast."

"I hope the boys are pleased then. I'm ready to go home and see me ma. It's been a while."

"It has, but all in a good cause."

"What about these AVNI people? Are we certain they aren't on our tails? I don't want to end up face down in a ditch at the last minute."

"Billy, don't worry. Once the money transfers it's too late for them to hurt the plan, and anyway we'll be back on home turf soon, where the boys can put security around us. If you want to see the city you'd better do it quickly."

Flaherty left to go and find a computer with Internet access and Billy decided he would just hang around the hotel. He had been in the lounge area reading a book for an hour or so when a smartly-dressed young man came across to him.

"Are you William Murphy by any chance?"

Billy put the book down. "That's me."

The stranger sat down opposite and opened a briefcase. He pulled out a thin plastic folder and handed it to Billy. "There you are, that's the standard recording contract we use for all new artists."

"Should I get a lawyer to look at it before I sign my life away?"

The man shrugged. "Suit yourself. Mr Christophides will drop you like a hot brick if you mess him around. My advice is to sign it now and renegotiate once you are successful. That gives you the upper hand later. In the meantime we will develop your career. The boss says we are going to market you as 'The Minstrel Boy'. Does that suit you?"

"You have a pen?"

He took the pen that was offered and signed the contract after filling in all the details needed. He handed the folder back and watched it vanish into the briefcase.

"A copy will be sent to the address you've put on here and a plan will come with it telling you how we are going to proceed."

"Do I get any input to that plan?"

"Frankly, no, that's not how Mr Christophides wants us to operate. Off the record and just between us, you will be looked after well enough, but as and when the big money starts to roll in you will get treated a whole lot better."

Billy leaned back in the hotel chair. "Well, that was short and sweet. I expected this to take a while."

"Not when Mr Christophides gives an instruction. When he says 'jump' we say 'how high?' No arguing with the boss if you want to keep your job."

The man clicked the catches on the shiny briefcase and stood up to go. "One more thing. I have a message for Mr Flaherty. Is he here?"

"No, but I can pass it on."

"Fair enough. Mr Christophides says that the other matter he agreed will be dealt with first thing Monday morning when the CFO gets back from vacation. Does that make sense?"

Billy nodded. "It does, thank you. I will pass that on when Paddy gets back."

The young man smoothed down his jacket, picked up the briefcase and, having nodded, walked towards the exit. Billy watched him go and as he turned back to his book he saw Flaherty coming towards him across the wide lobby.

"Who was that then?"

"Didn't get his name. He's some flunkey from the recording company. Brought me a contract to sign. It seems our friend doesn't let the grass grow under his feet when he makes a decision."

"So our payments should be in the bank anytime now then?"

"Not so. It seems he has to wait for the Chief Financial Officer to get back from his holidays. He sent a message to say the payments would happen first thing on Monday morning."

Flaherty sat down wearily. "Never mind, that's only a few days and he came through with your contract pretty damned fast. Anyway, the army council has told us to come home and I've booked the flights. We leave tomorrow. Norwegian Flight DY7152 to London Gatwick at

231

21:05 and then Easy Jet Flight EZY835 to Belfast. We should land in Ireland about four in the afternoon on Saturday. How does that sound?"

"I'll be glad to be home and bring this whole thing to a close."

Chapter 56

The rain streaked across the windows as Flight EZY835 made its final approach through the roiling clouds into Belfast. They touched down on the sodden runaway and Billy could see the spray flying out from the undercarriage. He looked out at the airfield as they trundled along the taxiway to the terminal and after the usual rush in the aisle he got his hand luggage out of the overhead bin and they walked into the arrivals hall.

The flight had only been about half full so the baggage came through to the carousel quickly and they made their way through into the main terminal.

"Taxis are that way, Billy," Flaherty said as he pointed.

"No need. My brother is here with a car to pick us up. There he is now."

Flaherty looked around and saw the tall, smiling man coming towards them. He flung his arms around Billy for a welcoming hug and then held out his hand to Flaherty.

"G'day, I'm Connor Murphy, Billy's little brother."

"Not so little anymore," Billy said as he looked up at his taller sibling.

"Nice to meet you. Is that right you've got a car for us?"

"Sure it is. Couldn't have my big brother standing in the rain looking for a cab, now, could I? It's over this way. I'll take the guitar if you like?"

They walked together out to the wide car park and Connor led them to the hire car he had ready. With the baggage loaded they drove through and out onto the main Belfast road.

"You can just drop me by my place on the way down here. That'll suit me fine well." Flaherty said.

Connor looked over his shoulder and smiled. "Ah no, surely not. There's someone waiting at ours who wants to meet you and she's made a cake for the tea."

"Why would your ma want to see me?"

"Oh, it's not Ma. She's away down to Dublin to see our uncle. No, it's our sister, Mary. You've not met her, have you?"

"No, I've never met her. Didn't you say she'd moved away, Billy?"

"I did indeed. She moved to the States and got herself a fine job there."

"A shame we didn't see her while we were there then."

"True enough, but we'll make up for it now."

They drove in to the city and Billy looked around with fresh eyes after his travels. The buildings looked tired and the streets were in need of a clean despite the rain that sluiced along the gutters.

"See, that's my street just there. You can drop me back there later, eh?"

Connor glanced up the side street with its kerbstones painted in the colours of the Southern

Irish flag. "Oh, right enough. I'll take you back there later, never fear."

They drove on and pulled up in the alley around the back of the house. Connor locked the car doors and they went in through the kitchen door and on into the front parlour.

"Sit down, Paddy, make yourself comfortable. You've been here before though, eh, when Seamus was alive?"

Flaherty looked around the room. "I may have visited him here. It's a long time ago and my memory isn't all it used to be, for sure."

Billy sat down opposite him and Connor stood by the fireplace. Mary came through carrying a tray of tea in mugs with a cake alongside them.

"And here we are all together for the first time in years," Billy said. "This is my big sister, Mary. She's one of the reasons we are here now, so it is."

Flaherty looked puzzled. "I don't get it. How do you mean?"

Billy smiled and glanced at his brother and sister. "You said your memory wasn't what it was. So let me refresh it for you."

He leaned forward and took a mug of tea, then leaned back and sipped it before he spoke. "Seamus Murphy wasn't my father. He made us call him 'Da' or we got a smack round the head and not a gentle one. Our father was Brendan Mulvaney, a good Catholic and a family man. He wanted nothing to do with the armed struggle and you people. He just wanted to raise his family in

235

this little house, and he worked hard to do just that. He made a huge mistake, though. He lived in a house that overlooked the army barracks and you people wanted that so you could track what they were doing in there. He refused to help, d'you remember that?"

"I remember something of it maybe," Flaherty said quietly.

"So the IRA decided an observation post was more important than our father and he was killed. Murdered and left face down in a ditch for some kids to find. Ma was beside herself with three kids to look after and no man. Then an old boyfriend from years before turned up and after a while she married him. Seamus bloody Murphy. One of your killers moved in with us."

"I don't see what this has to do with me. I think I'll go now."

Flaherty stopped as he heard the pistol cock and he looked to see the silenced automatic in Connor's hand. "No, you'll be staying to hear the whole story. We want you to know it all before you go. Go on, Billy."

"So yes, Murphy moved in and the beatings started. Anything he didn't like we got belted and Ma was too scared to stop him. She tried once and she got a beating and that was not the only time he hit her. He made our lives a living hell for your damned cause."

"Well, I'm sorry to hear that, but …"

"I haven't finished. It gets worse. Every Friday night Ma would go to the bingo down at the church hall and every Friday night Murphy would go into Mary's room. She was feckin twelve when he started, for God's sake, and we had to sit in our room and listen to it. Afterwards we'd go and sit with her while she cried her eyes out. Every bloody Friday."

"That's a tragedy, but ..."

"And then one night you came around here. Me and Connor were locked in the cupboard under the stairs for something we'd done or maybe just for fun. You and Murphy were sat in here drinking whiskey and bragging about the things you'd done. You two even bragged about killing our father to get access to the house. We just sat in the dark and listened and cried. We saw your face through the cracks in the door when you were leaving and we heard your voice loud and clear. I wasn't sure it was you to start with in that pub when we met, but then I heard your voice and I knew."

"Oh, now wait a minute ..."

"Now, my father's big old family bible was under the stairs with us and me and Connor swore an oath on it, to get our revenge one day. A kids' promise, but we didn't forget. Then you appeared and our chance had come. We'd already paid Murphy back when he was passed out drunk, you see. When we got big enough all three of us got him; we took turns slicing the message into his skin. Then we had the idea of those cards so the IRA and police would look another way. AVNI was for Army Veterans Northern Ireland and you thick shits fell for it. I was going to kill you, too, but then you gave us a gift, you introduced us to

237

more of your murdering kind and we got an even better revenge."

"You mean you …"

"No, not me. Mary took out the ones in the States and Connor got the ones in Australia. Oh that's right, you don't know yet. Molly and Sean are dead, thanks to Connor."

"But how did they track us? I made sure you never went near a phone or a computer."

"Ah yes, but you made sure I brought my old guitar, didn't you? There's a small pouch in the lining of the case that just fits a smart phone. So I could call in the cavalry whenever I went to bed. Oh, and I passed on the information about your codes to the police. They'll have been tracking your plans for a while now."

Flaherty raised a thin smile. "It doesn't matter. The armed struggle will start again without those martyrs. As soon as Christophides transfers the money tomorrow we'll be unstoppable and you'll be a dead man."

Billy smiled and looked at Mary. "You want to tell him?"

She smiled sweetly and sat down on the arm of Billy's chair. "The money won't be coming, Paddy. They are going to find Mr Christophides behind the dumpster outside his office block. He thought I found him attractive, or maybe he thought I wanted his money. Either way he was slobbering all over me when I stuck a gun in his face and pulled the trigger. He took three bullets to the head just to make sure and I shot him in the balls as well, before I gave him his AVNI card."

"Why would you kill him?"

"He was going to fund you murdering bastards and bring the misery back to this island again. We couldn't allow anyone else to feel what we had to go through because of you lot."

Flaherty sagged into his chair, the tea going cold beside him. "So now what?"

"Now you have to go and explain to the IRA army council just how badly you screwed up and see how they react."

"Get up. I'll take you back to your place now," Connor said, gesturing with the gun.

Flaherty stood and looked down at Billy. He was going to speak, but then just shook his head. He looked at Mary, who stared back at him in silence. He walked in front of Connor through the kitchen and into the back yard. The silenced pistol coughed once and he collapsed onto the stone flagged ground with a round through the back of the knee.

"Kneecapping's not so much fun when it's done to you, is it, Flaherty?"

"You said I could go!"

"And the man that killed my dad believed me? That's rich."

The pistol coughed again and Flaherty's other knee was destroyed by the .9mm round. He clutched at the ruined limb and moaned. The tears of agony rolled down his face as he looked around for help.

Connor stood over him and put another round into his head. He rolled him to one side and tucked a business card into his top pocket before

239

he and Billy loaded him into the car. They drove him out into the country to where a small stone memorial stood next to a filthy, water-filled ditch. They dragged the body out and, without ceremony, tossed it into the water.

For a moment they stood to get their breath back and watched the corpse as it sank below the surface, then Billy reached down and touched the memorial. "There you go, Dad. All done now."

The Minstrel Boy – Factual Content

In all my books I like to include a chapter at the end to give the reader a glimpse of the historical context so they can judge whether my story has done justice to the events described. This book is no exception to that rule and here it is.

All through the book I have inserted chapters that describe the terrorist atrocities carried out during what is euphemistically known as The Troubles. I have inserted fictional people into the action and given them leading roles. Obviously there is some poetic licence there, but the actual atrocities I describe took place and were as heartless and destructive as I hope I have been able to describe. If you doubt any of the incidents I have described please feel free to look them up on the Internet. I have been careful not to exaggerate any of the atrocities; in fact I may have underplayed the horror that was visited on the people in Northern Ireland during this conflict.

I have also described the naivety of people with Irish heritage who, for many years, were fed lies by the IRA and their apologists in order to obtain support and, more importantly, money from them. That money was given in good faith to support the people of Ireland, but it was not used that way. The money went to buy weapons and explosives and to finance terrorists who killed their fellow citizens with a startling lack of compassion. Children were targeted without a second thought, yet the perpetrators of these horrors portrayed themselves as some kind of heroes. The security forces were there to try and stop the violence and to protect the people of Northern Ireland. They, too, were attacked for no reason other than to try and create a united Ireland against the wishes of the majority of the people who lived in the north of that divided island.

The utter tragedy of the 9/11 terror attacks brought home to Americans the reality of terrorism. Maybe, just maybe, it has also opened their eyes to the facts of terror committed by the IRA, and others, in Ireland and elsewhere. I certainly hope so.

The Causes - See the end of the book

In researching this book I went looking for a description of how and why the Troubles started. In searching the Internet I found a number of explanations that stated that the IRA only started to target soldiers after the debacle of Bloody Sunday. This is an outright lie propagated by terrorists and their apologists. Bloody Sunday took place on the 30th January 1972. In 1971, for instance, 48 soldiers and 11 RUC officers were murdered by terrorists. Included in the 48 is Sergeant Michael Willets of the Parachute Regiment who deliberately sacrificed his life to protect civilians from a bomb blast. The information I have used for the epilogue comes from a far less biased source. Most of it was written by Jeff Wallenfeldt.

You can find the rest of the story at https://www.britannica.com/event/The-Troubles-Northern-Ireland-history

The Dedication

The dedication at the front of this book includes Sgt Stuart Reed of the Royal Electrical and Mechanical Engineers, killed in a landmine and gunfire attack on his Land Rover near Dungiven on June 24th 1972. As an army aircraft technician I had been working in a small repair team with Stuart Reed as my crew chief. I left the province on the Thursday and my crew were ambushed on the Saturday as they transported a helicopter for repair. L/Cpl David Moon and Pte Christopher Stevenson were also murdered in the same attack. Sgt Whitney and Cpl Grosvenor were both wounded.

The Atrocities

17th February 1978

The fire bomb at the La Mon restaurant near Belfast burned twelve people to death and severely injured thirty more. Some of those were still receiving treatment twenty years later. Robert Murphy was found guilty of the attack and was sentenced to twelve terms of life imprisonment. The attack was carried out by an IRA Active Service Unit (ASU) but only Murphy was caught. The IRA admitted responsibility for the attack and apologised for the inadequate warning. How that was supposed to make up for the atrocity is a puzzle.

4th February 1974

The coach bombing on the M62 Motorway took twelve lives, including two very young children. Others were seriously injured, including a six-year-old boy, who suffered severe burns. The investigation was botched and Judith Ward was charged and convicted on her own confession, despite the fact that she had mental health issues. The IRA issued a statement saying that she was not involved, but it was discounted in the rush for 'justice'. She was released in May 1992 having served almost eighteen years for a crime she never committed. Nobody else was ever charged for these twelve murders.

27th August 1979

Lord Louis Mountbatten had served in the armed forces with considerable distinction. Now 79 years of age, he was enjoying a quiet retirement when his boat was blown to pieces under him. Also killed was an 83-year-old woman and two boys aged fourteen and fifteen. The IRA gleefully claimed responsibility for the slaughter, admitting that it was a publicity stunt to get the attention of the British, who were trying to keep the peace in Northern Ireland. Thomas McMahon was jailed for the murders, but was released in 1988 under the terms of the Good Friday Agreement.

On the same day, at Warrenpoint on the border with the Republic, eighteen soldiers were slaughtered by a pair of hidden bombs. The explosions ripped men to pieces and body parts were scattered across the road, in the trees and in the water. One officer had to be identified by his face, which was recovered from the water after it had been ripped off his head by the blast. All that remained of the truck driver was his pelvis, which had been welded to his seat by the fierce heat. The Lieutenant Colonel who had taken command of the scene after the first attack, and was dealing with the wounded, was vaporised by the second bomb and only the epaulette of his jacket was found. Nobody was charged with the murders.

7 December 1972

Widowed mother of ten Jean McConville was taken from her flat in the Divis Flats complex in Belfast by four armed women. She was killed and her body was buried on Shellinghill Beach in the republic. The IRA denied responsibility for years, but later admitted the killing, claiming falsely that she had been an informant for the security forces. One of her sons was in the IRA and was imprisoned in the Long Kesh internment camp at the time of her murder. Some of her children were taken into care and suffered abuse. In particular, McConville's orphaned son Billy was sent to De La Salle Boys' Home, Rubane House, Kircubbin, County Down, notorious for child abuse, and suffered sexual and physical attacks from the staff.

5 January 1976

A red minibus was stopped on the road between Whitecross and Bessbrook by the IRA, who were masquerading as an army checkpoint. The twelve men inside, who were on their way home from work, were lined up and the lone Catholic was identified and sent on his way. The rest were gunned down at short range with automatic rifles. Ten of them died at the scene and were left in the road. One man miraculously survived with eighteen bullet wounds. Nobody has ever been arrested for the crime.

25th May 1971

Sergeant Michael Willetts was providing security in a police station on the Springfield Road in Belfast. A terrorist entered the building carrying a case which had a fuse burning on it. He dropped the case and ran away. The Sergeant, realising that this was a bomb, ushered people away from the device and then shielded them with his own body. He was fatally injured when the device exploded. He was jeered in the street when being carried out. He died two hours later in the Royal Victoria Hospital. This incident was the inspiration for the song "Soldier" by Harvey Andrews.

4th March 1973

Private Gary Barlow, of the Queen's Lancashire Regiment, was part of a search team in the Divis Flats in Belfast. At the end of the search the order was given to withdraw. For some reason Gary did not hear the order and as his unit moved out nobody noticed he was missing. He was surrounded by a large group of women who drove him back into a garage. He was held there until a killer was summoned to shoot him. He had declined to shoot the women to effect his own escape and his rifle had been taken from him by the time the killer arrived. He was 19.

26th October 1989

On 28 October 1989, IRA members opened fire on the car of RAF Corporal Mick Islania. The corporal had just returned to the car from a petrol station snack bar in Wildenrath. Also in the car were his wife Smita and their six-month-old daughter, Nivruti. Corporal Islania was hit by multiple rounds and died instantly; his daughter was killed by a single shot to the head. Smita Islania suffered shock.

2nd December 1993

Lance Bombardier Paul Garrett of the Royal Artillery was coming to the end of a three-day patrol. He was the last man in the patrol and was shot in the stomach as he walked passed Lir Gardens, Victoria Street, in Keady. The shot was fired from high ground on the Granemore road, 164 yards away. He died within six minutes from the massive wound caused by the Barrett sniper rifle, despite the attempts of a local nurse and doctor to save him. His family returned to Guyana shortly afterwards.

12th February 1997

Lance Bombardier Stephen Restorick was the last British soldier officially recognised as being murdered by the IRA in Northern Ireland. His death prompted anger and condemnation from all sides. The 23-year-old Restorick had been manning a vehicle checkpoint in Bessbrook, Co Armagh, when an IRA sniper opened fire. He was smiling and chatting to a local Catholic woman as he handed back her driving licence when he was shot through the back with a high-velocity Barrett rifle.

Lorraine McElroy, who was returning home from buying ice-cream for her two children, narrowly escaped with her life when the single bullet passed through Restorick's body, and skimmed her forehead. She rode in the ambulance with him, and watched him die.

20th July 1982

The Hyde Park bombing killed four soldiers of the Blues and Royals on ceremonial duties and seven of their horses. The nails wrapped around the bomb and the fragments of the car that the bomb was mounted in ripped huge wounds into the horses and men.

The bomb below the bandstand in Regent's Park killed seven men of the Green Jackets band that was entertaining the crowds of tourists. Eight civilians were wounded.

Additionally, eighteen soldiers, a policeman and three civilians were hospitalised, some with life-changing injuries. The horse called Sefton, although badly wounded, survived and became famous, being made Horse of the Year by a magazine. His rider was not so fortunate and suffered severe PTSD; he committed suicide some years later after killing two of his children. Another three deaths to lay at the feet of the IRA.

A memorial has been erected at the site of the atrocity and the cavalry troop honours it daily with an eyes left and salute with drawn swords.

The police were certain they knew who carried out the Hyde Park bombing and an individual from County Donegal was arrested. His trial at the Old Bailey collapsed when it was found he had been issued a letter by the Police Service of Northern Ireland stating that he would not be prosecuted for this crime. This was one of some 187 so called 'Letters of Comfort' issued to terrorists that guarantees them immunity from prosecution for their crimes.

10th March 1971

Three young soldiers from The Royal Highland Fusiliers, stationed in Girdwood Barracks in Belfast, were granted an afternoon pass to allow them to leave their base for some down time. They were unarmed and civilian clothes drinking in "Mooney's", a city centre bar. They were enticed into a car by a young woman with promises of a party. They stopped at White Brae off the Ligoniel Road for a comfort break and were murdered by the IRA. Two were shot in the back of the head and one in the chest. They were found, heaped on top of each other, by children at 9:30 that evening. The three young men were aged 17, 19 and 23 and two of them were brothers.

The memorial placed at the scene of the murders has been vandalised a number of times. No one has been charged with this atrocity.

6th March 1988

The IRA sent an active service unit of three volunteers to Gibraltar with instructions to bomb the changing of the guard ceremony. Had they been successful the number of deaths and injuries among the tourists watching the ceremony would no doubt have been considerable. They were unarmed when shot by an SAS team, but since a car they had hired was found just beyond the border with Spain, loaded with explosives, there can be no doubt that the actions of the SAS team saved many lives.

As usual, Sinn Fein politicians and the left wing media in the UK accused the SAS of murder, despite the clear evidence that the IRA had been stopped during the early stages of a planned atrocity.

19th March 1988

During the funeral of an IRA volunteer, a car containing two Corporals from the Royal Corps of Signals drove into the procession by mistake. One of the men was new in the province and it is thought that the driver was showing him around the city as orientation. They were dragged from the car and savagely beaten before being shot multiple times once they were unable to defend themselves. Two men were convicted for the murders, but were released early as part of the Good Friday Agreement. Others were convicted of lesser charges. Politicians on all sides in the UK and in the Republic of Ireland condemned the killings as an act of appalling savagery.

24th October 1990

Patrick Gillespie worked as a civilian cook at the Fort George army base to support his family. The IRA forced their way into his house and held his family at gunpoint with the promise that they would all die unless he drove the van. He did his best to warn the soldiers as he approached the checkpoint, but as he opened the door to shout more clearly 1000 pounds of explosive exploded. Five soldiers of the King's Regiment were killed. Gillespie's body was unrecoverable. He died on his son's 18th birthday. His crime? Supporting his family.

At his funeral Bishop Edward Daly said the IRA were 'the complete contradiction of

Christianity. They may say they are followers of Christ. Some may even still engage in the hypocrisy of coming to church, but their lives and their works proclaim clearly that they follow Satan.'

Author's Comment on Bloody Sunday

The incidents above were the ones I used in my fictional story. All are true and there are so many others I could have used. However, I would like to make a further point.

When speaking about the Troubles you will no doubt hear about Bloody Sunday and I have to agree the army did not cover itself in glory that day. The Parachute Regiment had been trying to contain a violent riot when they believed that they were fired upon. They returned fire and 28 people were shot; 14 of them died. Naturally the IRA and the Republican movement have made great play of this and at the time of writing are once again trying to indict one of the soldiers involved despite two major inquiries having taken place in the past.

I do not wish to downplay the tragedy of Bloody Sunday in any way, but maybe we should also consider the following:-

Bloody Monday - 31 July 1971 when the IRA murdered 9 people in Claudy.

Bloody Tuesday - 12 June 1972 when the IRA murdered 6 pensioners in Coleraine.

Bloody Wednesday - 13 July 1983 when the IRA murdered 4 UDR soldiers outside Omagh.

Bloody Thursday - 28 February 1972 when the IRA murdered 9 police officers in Newry.

Bloody Friday - 21 July 1972 when the IRA murdered 9 people in Belfast.

Bloody Saturday - 23 October 1993 when the IRA murdered 9 innocent people on the Shankhill Road in Belfast.

Two other Bloody Sundays

20 November 1983 when the INLA murdered 3 Protestants at their church in Darkley.

8 November 1987 when the IRA murdered 11 people on Remembrance Sunday in Enniskillen.

All soldiers during the Troubles were obliged to carry the infamous "Yellow Card" which gave them the Rules of Engagement for opening fire. They were told that provided they obeyed these instructions they would need have no concerns about the legality of shooting terrorists. Given the behaviour of successive British governments in the face of the persecution of ex-soldiers, it would appear that was yet another politician's lie.

Army Code No 70771

INSTRUCTIONS FOR OPENING FIRE IN NORTHERN IRELAND

General Rules

1. In all situations you are only to use the minimum force necessary. FIREARMS MUST ONLY BE USED AS A LAST RESORT

2. Your weapon must always be made safe: that is, NO live round is to be carried in the breech and in the case of automatic weapons the working parts are to be forward, unless you are ordered to carry a live round in the breech or you are about to fire.

Challenging

3, A challenge MUST be given before opening fire unless:

a. To do so would increases the risk of death or grave injury to you or any other person.

b. You or others in the immediate vicinity are being engaged by terrorists.

3. You are to challenge by shouting:

"ARMY: STOP OR I FIRE" or words to that effect.

Opening Fire

4.You may only open fire against a person:

a.If he* is committing or about to commit an act LIKELY TO ENDANGER LIFE, AND THERE IS NO OTHER WAY TO PREVENT THE DANGER. The following are some examples of acts where life could be endangered, dependent always upon the circumstances:

(1)   Firing or about to fire a weapon.

(2)   Planting detonating or throwing an explosive device (including a petrol bomb).

(3)   Deliberately driving a vehicle at a person and there is no other way of stopping him*.

b.If you know that he* has just killed or injured any person by such means and he* does not surrender if challenged and THERE IS NO THER WAY TO MAKE AN ARREST.

*"She" can be read instead of "he" if applicable.

6. If you have to open fire you should:

a. fire only aimed shots,

b. fire no more rounds than are necessary,

c. take all reasonable precautions not to injure anyone other than your target.

PP1/21271/11/80/BF   1.1.81

The Black Rose at 160 State Street in Boston is a rather fine Irish pub. If you ever go there, please tell them I sent you. It is also true that if you leave the Black Rose and walk towards the sea you find yourself next to 'Legal Sea Foods' and it really is an excellent restaurant if you like fish. The Marriott Long Wharf is a luxury hotel right on the harbour side in Boston and the bar and restaurant do have great views across the harbour.

If you are interested in finding out the truth of what went on in Northern Ireland during the so-called Troubles, then I recommend you look for books by Ken Warton. These are generally told from the soldier's point of view and demonstrate what the army went through to try and keep the peace. 'A Long Long War' is probably the best one to start with.

The Minstrel Boy
The Songs

The Minstrel Boy

The minstrel boy to the war is gone;
In the ranks of death you'll find him;
His father's sword he has girded on,
And his wild harp slung behind him.
"Land of Song!" said the warrior bard,
"Though all the world betrays thee,
One sword, at least, thy rights shall guard,
One faithful harp shall praise thee!"

The Minstrel fell! But the foeman's chain
Could not bring that proud soul under;
The harp he loved ne'er spoke again,
For he tore its chords asunder
And said, "No chains shall sully thee,
Thou soul of love and bravery!
Thy songs were made for the pure and free
They shall never sound in slavery!"

Kevin Barry

In Mountjoy jail one Monday morning,
High upon the gallows tree,
Kevin Barry gave his young life
For the cause of liberty.
Just a lad of eighteen summers,
Still there's no one can deny,
As he walked to death that morning,
He proudly held his head on high.
  Chorus
Shoot me like an Irish soldier.
Do not hang me like a dog,
For I fought to free old Ireland
On that still September morn
All around the little bakery
Where we fought them hand to hand,
  Chorus
Shoot me like an Irish soldier,
For I fought to free Ireland.
Just before he faced the hangman,
In his dreary prison cell,
British soldiers tortured Barry,
Just because he would not tell
The names of his brave comrades,
And other things they wished to know.
"Turn informer or we'll kill you."
Kevin Barry answered, "No,"
  Chorus
Proudly standing to attention
While he bade his last farewell
To his broken-hearted mother
Whose grief no one can tell.

For the cause he proudly cherished
This sad parting had to be,
Then to death walked softly smiling
That old Ireland might be free.
> *Chorus*
Another martyr for old Ireland,
Another murder for the crown,
Whose brutal laws may kill the Irish,
But can't keep their spirit down.
Lads like Barry are no cowards.
From the foe they will not fly.
Lads like Barry will free Ireland,
For her sake they'll live and die.

The Rising of the Moon

*"Oh then, tell me, Sean O'Farrell, tell me why you
hurry so?"*
*"Hush, mo bhuachaill, hush and listen," and his
cheeks were all aglow.*
*"I bear orders from the captain, get you ready
quick and soon,*
*For the pikes must be together at the rising of the
moon.*
*"I bear orders from the captain, get you ready
quick and soon,*
*For the pikes must be together at the rising of the
moon.*
*"O then, tell me, Sean O'Farrell, where the
gath'ring is to be?"*
*"In the old spot by the river, well-known to you
and me.*
*One word more for signal token, whistle up the
marchin' tune*
*With your pike upon your shoulder, by the rising of
the moon."*
*One word more for signal token, whistle up the
marchin' tune*
*With your pike upon your shoulder, by the rising of
the moon."*
*Out from many a mud wall cabin eyes were
watching through that night,*
*Many a manly heart was throbbing for the blessed
warning light.*
*Murmurs passed along the valleys like the
Banshee's lonely croon*
And a thousand blades were flashing at the rising

of the moon.

*Murmurs passed along the valleys like the
Banshee's lonely croon*

*And a thousand blades were flashing at the rising
of the moon.*

*There beside the singing river, that dark mass of
men were seen,*

*Far above the shining weapons hung their own
beloved green.*

*"Death to every foe and traitor! Forward! Strike
the marching tune!*

*And Hurrah, my boys, for Freedom! 'Tis the rising
of the moon.*

*"Death to every foe and traitor! Forward! Strike
the marching tune!*

*And Hurrah, my boys, for Freedom! 'Tis the rising
of the moon.*

*Well, they fought for poor old Ireland, and full
bitter was their fate;*

*Oh, what glorious pride and sorrow fills the name
of Ninety-Eight!*

*Yet, thank God, even still are beating hearts in
manhood's burning noon*

*Who would follow in their footsteps at the rising of
the moon.*

*Yet, thank God, even still are beating hearts in
manhood's burning noon*

*Who would follow in their footsteps at the rising of
the moon.*

Fields Of Athenry
by Paddy Reilly

By a lonely prison wall
I heard a young girl calling,
"Michael, they are taking you away
For you stole Trevelyn's corn
So the young might see the morn.
Now a prison ship lies waiting in the bay."
    [Chorus]
Low lie the Fields of Athenry
Where once we watched the small free birds fly.
Our love was on the wing, we had dreams and
songs to sing
It's so lonely 'round the Fields of Athenry.
By a lonely prison wall
I heard a young man calling,
"Nothing matters, Mary, when you're free.
Against the Famine and the Crown
I rebelled; they cut me down.
Now you must raise our child with dignity."
    [Chorus]
By a lonely harbour wall
She watched the last star falling
As the prison ship sailed out against the sky
For she'll live and hope and pray
For her love in Botany Bay
It's so lonely 'round the Fields of Athenry.
    [Chorus]

The Epilogue – The Causes

The Troubles, the euphemistic name for the violent sectarian conflict from about 1968 to 1998 in Northern Ireland between the overwhelmingly Protestant unionists (loyalists), who wanted the province to remain part of the United Kingdom, and the overwhelmingly Roman Catholic nationalists (republicans), who wanted Northern Ireland to become part of the Republic of Ireland. The other actors in the sad quarrel were the British army, Royal Ulster Constabulary (RUC), and Ulster Defence Regiment (UDR) and their purpose was to play a peacekeeping role. They faced the nationalist Irish Republican Army (IRA), which viewed the conflict as a guerrilla war for national independence, and the unionist paramilitary forces; both of which used aggression and terrorism. The conflict was marked by street fighting, sensational bombings, sniper attacks, roadblocks, and internment without trial, the confrontation had the characteristics of a civil war, notwithstanding its textbook categorization as a "low-intensity conflict." Some 3,600 people were killed and more than 30,000 more were wounded before a peaceful solution, which involved the governments of both the United Kingdom and Ireland, was effectively reached in 1998, leading to a power-sharing arrangement in the Northern Ireland Assembly at Stormont.

Although more than one violently disrupted political march has been pointed to as the starting point of the Troubles, it can be argued that the initiating event occurred on October 5, 1968, in Derry, where a march had been organized by the NICRA to protest discrimination and gerrymandering. The march was banned when unionists announced that they would be staging a counterdemonstration, but the NICRA decided to carry out their protest anyway. Rioting then erupted after the RUC violently suppressed the marchers with batons and a water cannon.

Also part of the initiation were the events surrounding a march held by loyalists in Londonderry on August 12, 1969. Two days of rioting that became known as the Battle of Bogside and stemmed from the escalating clash between nationalists and the RUC, which was acting as a buffer between loyalist marchers and Catholic residents of the area. Rioting in support of the nationalists then erupted in Belfast and elsewhere, and the British army was dispatched to restore calm. Thereafter, violent confrontation only escalated, and the Troubles began.

Initially, the nationalists welcomed the British army as protectors and as a balance for the Protestant-leaning RUC. In time, however, the army would be viewed by nationalists as another version of the enemy, especially after its aggressive efforts to disarm republican paramilitaries. In the process, the IRA became the purported defender of the nationalist cause. From its base in Ireland the IRA had mounted an ineffectual guerrilla effort in support of Northern Ireland's nationalists from 1956 to 1962, but, as the 1960s progressed, the IRA became less concerned with affairs in the north than with advancing a Marxist political agenda. As a result, a splinter group, the Provisional Irish Republican Army (Provos), which was prepared to use force to bring about unification, emerged as the champion of Northern Ireland's nationalists. Believing that their fight was a continuation of the Irish War of Independence, the Provos adopted the tactics of guerrilla warfare, financed partly by members of the Irish diaspora in the United States and later supplied with arms and munitions by the government of Libyan strongman Muammar al-Qaddafi. Unionists also took up arms, swelling the numbers of loyalist paramilitary organizations, most notably the Ulster Volunteer Force (UVF) and Ulster Defence Association UDA).

In an attempt to address nationalist grievances, electoral boundaries were redrawn more fairly, efforts were made to rectify discrimination in housing and public employment, and the B Specials were decommissioned. At the same time, the government of Northern Ireland responded to the growing unrest by introducing increasingly stringent security measures, including internment or detention without trial. The overwhelming majority of those arrested were nationalists.

As the 1970s progressed, rioting became more common in Belfast and Derry, bombings of public places (by both loyalists and republicans) increased, and both sides of the conflict perpetrated violent, deadly atrocities. Barbed wire laid by British soldiers to separate the sectarian communities evolved into brick and steel "peace walls," some of which stood 45 feet (14 metres) high, segregating loyalist and republican enclaves, most famously the Falls Road Catholic community and the Shankill Protestant community of Belfast.

On January 30, 1972, the conflict reached a new level of intensity when British paratroopers fired on Catholic civil rights demonstrators in Londonderry, killing 13 and injuring 14 others (one of whom later died). The incident, which became known as "Bloody Sunday," contributed to a spike in Provos recruitment and would remain controversial for decades, hinging on the question of which side fired first. In 2010 the Saville Report , the final pronouncement of a British government inquiry into the event, concluded that none of the victims had posed a threat to the troops and that their shooting had been unjustified. British Prime Minister David Cameron responded to the report by issuing a landmark apology for the shooting:

In all, more than 480 people were killed as a result of the conflict in Northern Ireland in 1972, which proved to be the deadliest single year in the Troubles. That total included more than 100 fatalities for the British army, as the IRA escalated its onslaught. On July 21, "Bloody Friday," nine people were killed and scores were injured when some two dozen bombs were detonated by the Provos in Belfast. Earlier, in March, frustrated with the Northern Ireland government's failure to calm the situation, the British government suspended the Northern Ireland Parliament and reinstituted direct rule by Westminster.

Beginning in the mid-1970s, the IRA shifted the emphasis of its "Long War" from direct engagements with British troops to smaller-scale secretive operations, including the bombing of cities in Britain—a change of tactics the British military described as a shift from "insurgency" to "terrorism." Similarly, the loyalist groups began setting off bombs in Ireland. Meanwhile, paramilitary violence at mid-decade (1974–76) resulted in the civilian deaths of some 370 Catholics and 88 Protestants.

I hope you have enjoyed this book and if so an honest review on Amazon, or wherever you bought the book, would be very much appreciated.

For more information about my books please visit my website.

http://www.nigelseedauthor.com/

Nigel Seed

Born in Morecambe, England, into a military family, Nigel Seed grew up hearing his father's tales of adventure during the Second World War which kindled his interest in military history and storytelling. He received a patchy education, as he and his family followed service postings from one base to another. Perhaps this and the need to constantly change schools contributed to his odd ability to link unconnected facts and events to weave his stories.

Nigel later joined the Army, serving with the Royal Electrical and Mechanical Engineers in many parts of the world. Upon leaving he joined the Ministry of Defence during which time he formed strong links with overseas armed forces, including the USAF, and cooperated with them, particularly in support of the AWACS aircraft.

He is married and lives in Spain; half way up a mountain with views across orange groves to the Mediterranean. The warmer weather helps him to cope with frostbite injuries he sustained in Canada, when taking part in the rescue effort for a downed helicopter on a frozen lake.

His books are inspired by places he has been to and true events he has either experienced or heard about on his travels. He makes a point of including family jokes and stories in his books to raise a secret smile or two. Family dogs make appearances in some of his stories.

Nigel's hobbies include sailing and when sailing in Baltic he first heard the legend of the hidden U-Boat base that formed the basis of his first book (V4 Vengeance) some thirty eight years later.

The Other Books by this author

Drummer's Call
Revenge of a Lone Wolf

Simon Drummer is on loan to a bio-warfare protection unit in the USA when the terror they fear becomes real. A brilliant Arabic bio-chemist is driven to bring an end to the suffering of his countrymen. He believes that the regime that oppresses them could not exist without the support of the US government and the weapons they furnish. He needs to bring the truth to the American people in a way that will grab their attention. So begins his journey to bring brutal death and understanding to the USA. And now Simon must help to find him and stop him.

The Jim Wilson Series

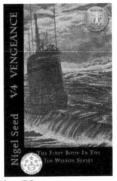

V4 – Vengeance

Hitler's Last Vengeance Weapons Are Going To War

Major Jim Wilson, late of the Royal Engineers, has been obliged to leave the rapidly shrinking British Army. He needs a job but they are thin on the ground even for a highly capable Army Officer. Then he is offered the chance to go to Northern Germany to search for the last great secret of World War 2, a hidden U Boat base. Once he unravels the mystery he is asked to help to spirit two submarines away from under the noses of the German government, to be the central exhibits in a Russian museum. But then the betrayal begins and a seventy year old horror unfolds.

Golden Eights
The Search For Churchill's Lost Gold Begins Again

In 1940, with the British army in disarray after the evacuation from Dunkirk, invasion seemed a very real possibility. As a precaution, the Government decided to protect the national gold reserves by sending most of the bullion to Canada on fast ships that ran the gauntlet of the U boat fleets. But a lot of gold bars and other treasures were hidden in England. In the fog of war, this treasure was lost. Now, finally, a clue has emerged that might lead to the hiding place. The Government needs the gold back if the country is not to plunge into a huge financial crisis. Major Jim Wilson has been tasked to find it. He and his small team start the search, unaware that there is a traitor watching their every move and intent on acquiring the gold, at any cost.

Two Into One
*A Prime Minister Acting Strangely and World
Peace in the Balance*

Following his return from Washington the
Prime Minister's behaviour has changed. Based on
his previous relationship with the PM, Major Jim
Wilson is called in to investigate. What he finds is
shocking and threatens the peace of the world. But
now he must find a way to put things right and
there is very little time to do it. His small team sets
out on a dangerous quest that takes them from the
hills of Cumbria to the Cayman Islands and Dubai,
but others are watching and playing for high
stakes.

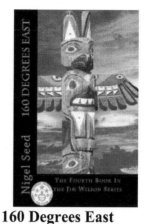

160 Degrees East

A fight for survival and the need to right a terrible wrong.

Major Jim Wilson and his two men are summoned at short notice to Downing Street. The US Government has a problem and they have asked for help from Wilson and his small team. Reluctantly Jim agrees, but he is unaware of the deceit and betrayal awaiting him from people he thought of as friends. From the wild hills of Wales to the frozen shores of Russia and on to the mountains of British Columbia Jim and his men have to fight to survive, to complete their mission and to right a terrible wrong.

One More Time

*A Nuclear Disaster Threatened By Criminals Must
Be Prevented At All Costs*

Jim and Ivan have retired from the Army and are making their way in civilian life when they are summoned back to the military by the new Prime Minister. Control of two hidden nuclear weapons has failed and they have been lost. Jim must find them before havoc is wreaked upon the world by whoever now controls them. It is soon apparent the problem is far bigger than originally envisaged, and there is a race against time to stop further weapons falling into the hands of an unscrupulous arms dealer and his beautiful daughter. The search moves from Zimbabwe to Belize and on to Norway and Spain, becoming ever more urgent and dangerous as the trail is followed.

Twelve Lives
A Threat to Millions But This Time It's Personal

During a highly classified mission for the British Government, Jim Wilson and his two companions make a dangerous enemy. A contract has been put on their lives and on those of their families. Jim moves the intended victims to safety and sets about trying to have the contract cancelled. However, his efforts to save his family uncover a horrendous plot to mount a nuclear terror attack on the United States and the race is on to save millions of lives.

North of Fifty Four
A Crime Must Be Committed To Prevent A War

Jim Wilson is forced to work for a Chinese criminal gang or his wife and child will be murdered. While he is away in the north of Canada, his wife manages to contact Ivan and Geordie for help. The two friends set out to save all three of them, but then the threat to many more people emerges and things become important enough to involve governments in committing a serious crime to prevent a new war in the Middle East.

Backpack 19

Nigel Seed

A Lost Backpack and a
World of Possibilities.

Backpack 19

A Lost Backpack and a World of Possibilities.

An anonymous backpack lying by the side of the road. Who picks it up and what do they find inside? There are many possibilities and lives may be changed for the better or worse. Here are just nineteen of those stories.

The Michael McGuire Trilogy

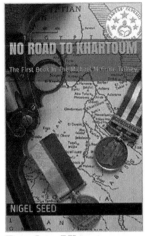

No Road to Khartoum

From the filthy back streets of Dublin to the deserts of the Sudan to fight and die for the British Empire.

Found guilty of stealing bread to feed his starving family, Michael McGuire is offered the "Queen's Hard Bargain", go to prison or join the Army. He chooses the Army and, after training in Dublin Castle, his life is changed forever as he is selected to join the 'Gordon Relief Expedition' that is being sent south of Egypt to Khartoum, in the Sudan.

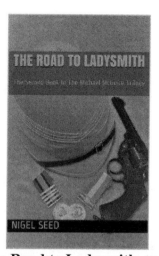

The Road to Ladysmith

*Only just recovered from his wounds Captain
McGuire must now sail south to the confusion and
error of the Boer War.*

After his return from the war in the Sudan,
McGuire had expected to spend time recovering
with his family. It was not to be, and his regiment
is called urgently to South Africa to counter the
threat from the Boers. Disparaged as mere farmers
the Boers were to administer a savage lesson to the
British Army.

The Bloody Road

Michael McGuire has left the army, but as the First World War breaks out his country calls him again.

At the start of the war the British expand their army rapidly, but there is a shortage of experienced officers and McGuire is needed. He is sent to Gallipoli in command of an Australian battalion that suffers badly in that debacle. He stays with them when their bloody road takes them to the mud and carnage of the western front.

If you have enjoyed this book a review on Amazon.com would be very welcome.

Please visit my website at www.nigelseedauthor.com for information about upcoming books.

Printed in Poland
by Amazon Fulfillment
Poland Sp. z o.o., Wrocław

54400274R00159